Memories of the Assassination Attempt
and Other Stories

Gerard Windsor

Gerard Windsor was born in Sydney in 1944 into a
medical family. He spent twenty years under the
educational care of the Jesuits and later took degrees at
both the Australian National University and Sydney
University. He has written an unpublished school
history, worked as a university tutor, and is currently
employed by the Special Broadcasting Service. His
reviews and articles have appeared widely in the
Sydney Morning Herald, the *Age* and the *Australian*,
and he reviews regularly for the *Bulletin*. His first
collection of stories, *The Harlots Enter First*, was
published in 1982.

D1630815

Gerard Windsor

MEMORIES OF THE ASSASSINATION ATTEMPT AND OTHER STORIES

PENGUIN BOOKS

Published with the assistance of the
Literature Board of the Australia Council

Penguin Books Australia Ltd,
487 Maroondah Highway, P.O. Box 257
Ringwood, Victoria, 3134, Australia
Penguin Books Ltd,
Harmondsworth, Middlesex, England
Penguin Books,
40 West 23rd Street, New York, N.Y. 10010, U.S.A.
Penguin Books Canada Ltd,
2801 John Street, Markham, Ontario, Canada L3R 1B4
Penguin Books (N.Z.) Ltd,
182-190 Wairau Road, Auckland10, New Zealand

First published by Penguin Books Australia, 1985

Typeset in Goudy Old Style by Leader Composition Pty. Ltd.
Made and printed in Australia by
The Dominion Press–Hedges & Bell

Publication assisted by the Literature Board of the Australia
Council, the Federal Government's arts funding and advisory body

CIP

Winsdor, Gerard
  Memories of the assassination attempt and other stories.

  ISBN 0 14 008558 0.

  I. Title.

A823'.3

For my parents

ACKNOWLEDGEMENTS

Acknowledgement is made to the publications in which these stories first appeared:

'The Sad Music of Men', *Island Magazine*, 1/1983

'Wedding Presents for Breakfast', *Quadrant*, October 1983

'Memories of the Assassination Attempt', *Bulletin*, 27 Dec. 1983/3 Jan. 1984

'The Archbishop or the Lady', *Meanjin*, 2/1984

'Reasons for Going into Gynaecology', *Southerly*, 3/1984

'A Real Little Marriage-Wrecker', *Fiction and Poetry Journal*, November 1984

'In the House of the Dead', *Westerly*, 4/1984

'The Victoria Cross of Timothy O'Hea', *Island Magazine*, 1/1985

'Can These Bones Live?', *Australian Literary Magazine*, 6/7 April 1985

'Far on the Ringing Plains', *Overland*, 1/1985

'My Father's Version of the Nurses' Story', *Meanjin*, 2/1985

The author is grateful for the assistance of a General Writing Grant from the Literature Board of the Australia Council.

CONTENTS

Memories of the Assassination Attempt   1
Far on the Ringing Plains   13
Reasons for Going into Gynaecology   25
The Sad Music of Men   37
Press Conferences of Ambassador Sweeney   49
Can These Bones Live?   61
Domestic Interludes:
    Wedding Presents for Breakfast   71
    Edging Around the Fat Man   81
In The House of the Dead   95
The Life of a Man's Man   107
A Real Little Marriage-Wrecker   125
Addendum to the First Fleet Journals   137
The Victoria Cross of Timothy O'Hea   145
The Archbishop or The Lady   157
My Father's Version of the Nurses' Story   173

MEMORIES OF THE ASSASSINATION ATTEMPT

Every day, when I raise the Host, I see the air torn, and the small loaves and the steaming gobbets of flesh tumbling, tumbling around me. There is nothing fragile or mortal about the picture. I can neither spoil nor ameliorate it. It hangs forever in the gallery of my mind, or my imagination. Each day at that moment I am yanked before it, held down in front of it. Once again I forcibly absorb the devastation and the shriek that explode from it.

Yet I search for the fragments. If I deal with them one by one, I tell myself, the picture might fade. If I can find a new pattern and install a new picture . . .

Mr Lincoln's America is no answer. Nor was that of Mr Jefferson. I was brought here by nothing more exalted than my own need for safety. I now know that my death would not have been at all fruitful. It could never have redressed or adjusted anything. But at that time, with the creatures of Bonaparte sniffing their way to the perimeters of France, I was not concerned by the larger patterns of my life or death. I wanted refuge. And the United States lay open.

Only when I knew I had life, and the vast portion of my

3

life, secure to me, only then did I wonder how it was to balance the dead weight of that one past instant. There was no other question for me. I have had no reason to open my eyes on America. I merely lurched far enough to be out of the more jostled paths of colonising and transient Frenchmen. I came here to Baltimore, to the seminary. I came here, a man under shock, guided by instinct, and with no sharp clarity of intention. Père le Chevalier de Limoëlan has a most particular vocation, the authorities here have explained to the students for sixty years.

My animosity towards Bonaparte is a dead memory. The feeling is quite beyond recall. I remember a virulence that wears the face of a grotesque snarl, but it has nothing to do with me. It belongs to a dog, it is remote, quite contemptible and absurd. The problem is that I can now find no proportionate reason for such a dedication to bitterness. I can rehearse the old shibboleths, but I laugh or I twitch with embarrassment at the hollow vanity of them. The besmirched glory of France, the enslavement of God's Church, the tyranny of alien, inferior blood. All ridiculous. Not the principles themselves, or at least not always, not necessarily. But as an adequate summary of Bonaparte's doings, they are laughably dishonest. There must have been some awful vortex of blood in the brain to ridge Bonaparte into such a corkscrewed, disposable shape. For he stained less than the regicides who preceded him: France's glory – ambivalent a notion as ever – owes more to him than to anybody: my own pride would not let the blood of the de Limoëlans freeze into submission before non-commissioned, Corsican riff-raff. How many other impurities and misjudgements made up the recipe for righteous wrath? Bonaparte managed another seventeen years after our attempt, and the world has survived him for nearly fifty years now. And who is to say whether his earlier absence would have made for better or worse?

All I remember is our certainty. How can anyone be so certain, least of all so murderously? Good versus evil, we tell ourselves, the good must take up arms and wage war tirelessly against the evil. And I believe it, but hardly in the same way now. There are no good men and evil men. Humanity does not divide that way. Very probably there are some that are more or less one or the other. Marginally. And beyond differentiation. What price then the arrogance of a de Limoëlan against the blasphemy of a Bonaparte? And what fee the wisdom of Solomon, unclouded by self-interest, to distinguish between the two? There are no laudable crusades. But there is good and there is evil, and war between them must be relentless.

'But what kind of horse?'

'Nothing special really. Just something cheap.'

The man wiped his hands slowly down his leather apron. There was contempt in the gesture. He turned half away. I knew he was right. I had a maladroit touch for this kind of activity. I had thought to be undemanding, unremarkable. I can assure you, I said in my mind to the dealer, that I am a little more knowledgeable, a little more fastidious, on the matter of mounts than you might suppose. The de Limoëlans have long taken pride in their stable. It was perverse to approach the man as though I were trying to relieve him of the ordure in these stables for the meanest possible price.

'What do you want it for?' the man asked.

'A procession,' I told him.

'A pageant is it?'

'More or less. I want an animal that's docile, not frightened by crowds, or applause. And that can draw a certain weight.'

The man sauntered into the darker interior of his stables.

'All the animals I have will do that.' A resolve to close the matter appeared in his voice. 'Cheap then, you say?'

'I have no wish to invest in the animal.' I was ashamed almost as I said it. Our resources were hardly so pinched. And so palpably inferior a sacrificial victim demeaned the occasion. Bonaparte is worth no more, I told myself savagely. I pointed to the listless beast nearest me. 'Name a price for this one,' I said.

The man gave me a surly stare. 'You want her?' he asked.

I yanked at the purse-strings. 'I have need of her,' I told him.

From the corner of the Rue Saint Nicaise I stared at the gates of the Tuileries. I was nauseous with longing that he should not come. They had arranged for him – for Bonaparte, First Consul, Master of Europe – some nameless 'they' had arranged – as though his nights could be dictated by non-entities . . . For this first Christmas Eve of a new century they had arranged his presence at old maestro Haydn's concert, at his *Creation*. Surely Bonaparte had his own worlds to fashion and arrange. Surely his murderous quicksilver would not settle down to the ponderous birth pangs of some old Austrian. Campaigns to plan, mistresses to attend to . . .

I tugged at the host of reasons why he should not come. And I threw quick, transparently suspicious glances down the Rue Saint Nicaise to where the disguised, blunt instrument of death was stationed. But it had not evaporated, and I could see the head of the fanatic Carbon, and I could imagine nothing but the impassive resolution of his features, obscured only by the premonitory puffs of smoke rising from his pipe. So I stared, stared at the closed gates of the Tuileries; my eyes gripped the cross-bolt, and froze, froze the ironwork into perpetual rest. And the concentration and the pressure set a tumult racing through my brain, so that all I could hear was the storming cry 'Stay there!' fuelled by greater hatred than ever for Bonaparte, and a white craving for his perdition, earthly and eternal, and the knowledge that any death he would now suffer would be hallowed or at least not universally applauded, and that I, above all, would be the cause.

So, as if through a screen, breaking into my dreams irrupted the jangle of escort and carriages. Out they swept, with peremptory ease, trampling on all my vain logic. 'Now' came the challenge from the neighing, snorting stallions and the arrogant cuirassiers, secure in the clanking of their sabres and spurs. The cavalcade of Bonaparte, punctual to the second, prancing at its regular, unbroken trot, whipping me across the mouth and sneering 'We'll accommodate you, you and your planning'. And they delivered themselves to me, and I had only to raise my left hand and hold it there till I saw the head, and the pipe, of Carbon bob down to their equally simple task. And the time for the proud, measured progress of Bonaparte was the length of the chosen fuse. And the cavalcade wheeled, directly in front of the Tuileries, and it was now.

But I could not raise my arm. Out of the darkness appeared a flicker of innocence, and it held me. And I found I was hardly even straining against such gravity. I would not stain my hand. I would keep it clean. I would let Bonaparte live for the sake of those who had not forfeited all rights as he had. I stood quite still and stared in proud triumph as the cavalcade bumped and tossed its way down the Place du Carrousel towards me. Quite pathetic they were, rattling and clattering round the corner into the Rue Saint Nicaise. The powdered, gaudy bullies bouncing in eternal complacency; the snaffling, goaded beasts in their futile rush; the woman, her child the randomly fathered Hortense, all wanton shoulders and a vacant giggle; and a scowling Bonaparte. Poor creatures rushing forward to the *Creation*, unaware that a power above their own had let them live a little longer. My hands trembled and held one another over my stomach, and I breathed in victory. I will wash my hands among the innocent.

'Nothing . . . nothing left to chance,' murmured Carbon. There was just the smallest trace of a question in his voice. Then his eyes came to rest on the horse. 'The animal might become restless, or take fright.'

'Tether it,' I said. 'There's a stanchion in the wall there.'

'It might just create suspicion, a horse and cart unattended, at this spot.' He looked at me, in the most casual way. 'Find someone to hold it,' he instructed.

There were enough human shards around. I approached a one-legged beggar, but he wanted to talk of Valmy and the salvation of the Republic and other endless drivel – all with a view to alms. So I hung on to the few coins, because he was too garrulous and complicated and dangerous, and I seized on a stinking hag. But she was quite deranged, and affected great affront that I was trying to buy her favours. A male, in much the same condition, was disqualifyingly drunk. And the crowd, sensing the imminent arrival of the great man, had swelled, and I could not see any lone individual to single out and approach quietly. I returned to Carbon, and shrugged at him across the cart. He simply pointed.

It was a young girl, about fourteen years of age. She was selling small loaves of bread, carrying them in a basket over her arm, and calling out, in an oddly cheerful voice, her wares and prices. Under Carbon's eye I opened my palm before her, held out the price of all she had in the basket, shook my head: no I wanted no bread; would she just hold a horse for me? And I nodded towards the animal.

The girl seemed to forget me. She rushed to the cart, set her basket down by the wheel, and stroked and nuzzled the horse, nestling her face in its mane and speaking to it as though it were her own long-separated child. She was oblivious to me or to the man Carbon appraising her from the other side of the cart. I walked across and dropped the few coins into the basket among the loaves. I did not look at her again, nor at the cart, nor at the still, set face of Carbon. I turned away towards my post at the entrance to the Rue Saint Nicaise.

Living like a rat in the Vendée. Merely an agent of destruction, a perpetrator. Neither a hero nor a martyr. Squeezed, like an infection, out of France, blown willy-nilly to the United States. I had time to think it over, reassess the attempt, let my mind trace the pattern and the shape it had taken. And a parody, a mockery emerged. There was nothing factitious about it. The one great story was never so much the warp of my life at that time that I should break into violent flushes at the least hint of any perversion or obscene mimicry of it. No, every step I had taken seemed to have its paradigm. But each time some malignant twist had been insinuated. Or, more accurately, I, acting under some force I cannot account for, provided that twist. And the sum of what I did was destruction. How could I knit anything together again? My own mind lurched about, somehow impaired, perhaps blinded, maimed.

I had to come here. There has never been any idea of making reparation. Life is taken away. We have no power to put it back, nor create new life that somehow replaces and compensates. Any programme of restoration is quite beyond me. For sixty years now I have been doing the only thing that has ever seemed possible. Revert to the paradigm. Keep attending to it, repeating it, performing it, and perhaps . . . I can be no more sure than that. And perhaps, through some force that is certainly not mine, the parodies, the perversions will become less and less likely to break out. Perhaps.

But I know that I was not born to bring salvation to any oppressed people. I had no business to requisition an ass for anyone's entry into the new Jerusalem. Purifying my hands as I passed judgement on humanity limping past deceived no one, except, momentarily, myself. And most evil, most terrifying of all, by what aberration did I take up the role of the angels, and approach a virgin, and ask her to be the instrument of my plan?

So the cavalcade whirled into the Rue Saint Nicaise. Carbon's face pointed towards me, still waiting. From where I stood I imagined I saw the start on his face as the first horses broke into his sight. I can see the expression, bewildered, enraged, torn. I would never be seeing him again. The man and his petty conspiracies were irrelevant. I watched his instant of glory collapse before it could flicker. Bonaparte was beyond his power.

And even as I watched his impotence, the man acted. Rage, panic, some access of stupidity engulfed him. I saw the hand go to the bowl of the pipe, and the man bob down, and then, after a few seconds, I saw him walking rapidly from the cart. I was transfixed. I could do nothing. My eyes were tied to the girl. She turned her head at the sound of the cavalcade, but she must have sensed some slight unease in the horse, for her stroking hand settled on its jaw, by the bit, and seemed to turn its head to look at her. She seemed oblivious to the royal progress until it had passed. Her head did not move, and, if she paid any attention at all, it was done without disturbing the attitude of love. As the last of the bobbing escort turned from sight towards the Opera, the bomb burst. Loaves and the severed head of a horse and the relics of a young girl raining into the gutters of Paris.

I whisper over the bread and it becomes the young girl's flesh and again I lift her up. And I pray to her as the flash and the roar of the moment rage through my skull.

FAR
ON THE
RINGING
PLAINS

Every year, on the anniversary, Austin wrote to me. He never mentioned that it was the anniversary. He never referred to the event that the family commemorated on that day, and, in any case, the letters only started after our parents had both died. My mother and father never saw Austin again after he left for Canada en route to Britain at the end of 1940. They had not heard from him since the death of our middle brother, Vince, three years later. We knew Austin was in England. We kept writing to him through the Air Force, but he never answered, and after the war we no longer had any address. No doubt he could have been tracked down, but the family didn't seem to have the will for it. Austin had made it quite clear he no longer wanted communication with us; my parents were both, in a very real way, enfeebled by the death of Vince, and they swung their affections totally onto what was near at hand, namely myself. And I was still a young schoolboy when the others went off to the war. I grew up and had to go to university, and get started in life, and I couldn't set off for the other side of the world to track down a very probably eccentric brother. Fantastic as it might have seemed to me as a child, families learn to cut their losses. Members are lost but the remainder cauterize themselves and close up and live for all the world as though their diminished state were the original one.

So we had. Till there was only me, and then there began the evolution of a new tribe that had very little connection with the old.

So the first communication was a totally alien, as well as unexpected, object. And in a variety of ways it kept its own reticent distance. It was a postcard, of the most proletarian and tasteless variety, a John Hinton production, printed in Singapore, of basic, saccharine colours, all overflowing their appropriate margins. The scene was not even identified, but called simply 'a typical English village'. The address was as notable for its incompleteness as for its eccentricity. At the top Austin had written 'Tower House', and then the date. He took up *in medias res*, but without any nod to my complete ignorance of the earlier part of his story, or any hint that he would return to a chronological order. I was made to feel a confidant, but one who had been out of the room while a garrulous, unnoticing old man had delivered his most critical and intimate disclosures.

My very dear young brother,
Retirement here should give me the chance to get things in perspective. The location, leisure, and the presence of my books all make for the ideal setting in which to stake out my best view of the matter. The winter was mild, and I feel buoyant about prospects.
    With affectionate regards,
        Austin

'Who is this man?' said my wife when I showed the card to her. She knew of course, but I took her point. Austin was not in the business of giving much away.

In a manner of speaking he was more expansive the following year.

It has not been a good winter. The Tower does not suit the books. Nor, for that matter, do books suit the Tower. Which was rather against the law of things, at least as I had always been led to believe in it.

I had imagined it was a good stock. It filled the building. I could wander from room to room, and enjoy the tug of interests that held me now in one, now in another place. I could linger over the stacks in the stairwells as my eye caught the titles edging past it. I could use the books to distract or stimulate me as I wished. On top of that they would bring me company, just as much as I needed to stave off complete solitude. A name like Tower House would appeal to the booklover. I would find them dropping in, but just as randomly as I was ambushed by the spines and titles of my collection. The visitors would appear and wander unchecked through all my rooms, and I could enjoy the sounds of their steps and their subdued comments and consultations, and please myself whether I had anything to do with them. And finally they would give me money, for they would feel they had trespassed if they went away without buying anything.

But no, it has not been a good winter. I refused to order my books in any system, and the visitors have tended to express exasperation and summarily walk out. There have been few enough of them in any case. The Tower is said to be isolated. 'You are rather inaccessible,' my visitors tell me. 'Off any routes, and not quite what we were looking for.'

Apart from that, the Tower has become excruciatingly cold. After all it was not designed for residential purposes. Draughts course wilfully up and down the stairwells. I am forced to wear gloves, even to bed, and that impedes my ability to handle the books, to say nothing of caressing or enjoying them. The books too have reacted. Overnight, with the universal efficiency of an Egyptian plague, damp has broken out. Books have buckled and curled and taken on a soggy quality, and the flat smell of stale, dusty moisture hangs in the air.

I have tried makeshift fires. The Tower was made without any provision for such comforts. By spooning out declivities and knocking out apertures I created a semblance of hearths here and there. The fuel suggested itself. The land for miles around the Tower was, of course, completely levelled thirty-odd years ago. In any case, distasteful as the Tower can be much of the time, the countryside – if one can call it that – has absolutely no winter attractions whatsoever. So I have started burning the books, those at the lower end of my market. Books make poor fuel, my books at any rate. They provide the flames with little more nourishment than they have given me. They content themselves with behaving like certain animals. Attacked, they give off a stench. In this case it is the rank, rotten smell of smoke.

Wherewith he signed himself off. The letter seemed incomplete.

'Writer interrupted?' asked my wife. 'A person from Porlock?'

'I wouldn't presume to deduce anything,' I answered.

Twelve months later I felt no more presumptuous.

I am looking forward to summer again. Last year the season was most productive, and if things go on that way, the place should be cleared eventually. The ideal would be one massive order. I imagine that by now somebody must have come up with a device that lifts off and rolls concrete or tar surfaces in the way that turf is handled. Might there not be a market in Australia, amongst the Returned Servicemen's clubs or similar organisations, for the stuff? I seem to recall that the Imperial Services Club down in Pitt Street always looked fairly flush – the sort of place that could well be in the market? Would you, like a good fellow, scout round, and see what you can come up with? It'd be a favour I'd be grateful for. The idea would never have occurred to me if it hadn't been for the summer rush. A few Canadians at first, and then Australians, in droves – by my standards at any rate. Initially they were very tentative. I watched them from the Tower, checking the area out, getting their bearings, half imagining that all the old security checks still applied. Women and children with them more often than not, looking dismayed. I wouldn't blame them. Usually they cottoned on to something that betrayed my presence – washing on the line, fresh rubbish, things of that nature. So they sought me out and asked. 'Could I just take a lump of the old runway? Not too much, just a small piece as a memento, for old times sake?'

'Go for your life,' I said to them. 'Take all you want. You can have the lot as far as I'm concerned.' None of them ever took me up, but the word might get around, and likely as not they'll be back in force this year and start shipping it out in a big way. All the same I'd be grateful for anything you could tie up out there. I don't see much profit in it for myself, but all the same the idea should have commercial attractions. There's no finesse needed in the handling or packaging, and it could have institutional appeal – to War Memorials, clubs etc. – after all we could probably manage some sort of discount for heavy orders – as well as to just the simple returned man.

I made no comment when I showed this letter to my wife. She was, I must say, very tactful. 'I didn't know there was any entrepreneurial spirit in your family,' she remarked. I suspect she would have left the matter there, but I needed to elicit a more profound reaction. 'Do you think he's mad?' She began to shrug at the prospect of venturing herself onto that topic. 'No, no,' I said, 'just from your knowledge of him through these letters?'

She considered a moment. 'What were his interests?' she asked.

'I've no idea,' I told her. 'He was an adult and I was a boy.'

One memory slipped back. 'Stamps. At least he had a stamp album.'

'I don't know,' said my wife. 'Maybe there's something of the magpie . . . but not all that much. He seems to be as interested in turnover as he is in accumulation. But why doesn't he stick to the one thing? I wonder whether he's got his heart in any of this. Perhaps his attention is really somewhere else. These letters,' she said and gestured wonderingly at the latest, 'they seem to speak by silences.'

The following year I am not sure that what we received from Austin was a letter at all. An envelope addressed to us arrived all right, but the sheets of paper it contained had neither address, date, salutation, introduction, nor valediction. The only ornament to the bald essay – for that's what it turned out to be – was at the end, the particularly carefully written signature *Austin Donnelly*.

They returned in quick succession. Breaking through the cloud of silence that stretched from the perimeter of the drome to the heart of Germany, they came back to us. One by one, roaring in, they confirmed the prediction for a quiet raid. Light flak, thin fighter defences – forecast, and realised.

I sat in the Tower, before the great sheet of window, and willed each of them to speak. Out they came, and declared themselves, and the letters of the alphabet marked themselves in, and the shape of the whole began to emerge again – Nectar, Sugar, King, Love, Jig, Ovo, Abel, Easy . . . But I was waiting. I had to be quite passive. Like a woman at the phone, I had to wait till they rang me. They spoke and I acknowledged, and I beckoned them forward, or I held them back, as gently and briefly as I could, sensing in each of them the animal impatient for its stable. Down they came, Charlie, William, Item . . . and still I waited.

Then I heard him – Vince. 'B Baker, calling Control. Clearance to land?' There was no need to hesitate or delay him: 'Control to B

Baker. Clearance to land.' I paused, and repeated, 'Clearance to land, B Brother'. And then, I know, I heard myself exhale with the release of tension, and I had to yank my concentration back to the rest of the squadron.

Between clearance call and touchdown there were barely thirty seconds, and as I turned my attention to the remaining calls I watched for Vince to taxi past. Yet again I felt the rope between brother and brother, taut and strong, registering its hold at the centre of this clamorous, chaotic enterprise, rendering it not just an adventure, not even just an invincible crusade, but a saga of my own blood and my own tribe. And so the rhythm passed over me, the rope tightening and spelling out my stability, and then relaxing. And I listened for the next call.

And the eruption of sound came. That was it really. There was little more than sound to it. Even as my own words hung in the air, a prolonged call because they were a call to a brother, other sounds reached them, and used them as a bridge. Alien sounds: engines that did not belong to the Halifaxes, roaring at full acceleration; the whoosh and crackle of aircraft cannon; the hurtle of a Junkers 88 as it sprinted past the Tower, hugging the ground, in the path of its own green tracers. And in its wake, the final sound of all, momentarily suspended, the scream of B Baker, already in flames and out of control, taking the full impact of the rearing, concrete earth and exploding.

'D Dog,' came the call of the next aircraft. 'Clearance to land?'

'Control to D Dog,' I managed to say, 'intruders, intruders. Get down and get out. Fast.' I took off the headphones and walked away. I wouldn't say anything else. Already I had said five words too many. The sky has ears, and five words of greeting were an invitation to death. Calling a brother out of the night sky, in the brief moment of his own sightlessness, prolonging the caress, to land him, incinerated, at my feet.

'Did you know about this?' my wife asked.

'No,' I told her. She left me alone.

The following year, when the letter came, she had more to say.

Ralph old chap,

I can't for the life of me remember what I told you in my last letter. So I won't try and pick up whatever threads there may have been.

We're in, I'm sure, for an exceptional spring. I had a most convincing intimation of this yesterday afternoon. This year, for the first time in my experience, green should be the predominant colour for miles around the Tower. The shoots are everywhere, in places they have not been seen for over thirty years. The prospects are good, and we all seem to be responding to it. The hunt was due to go out yesterday, and I was in a state of some excitement that I might catch a glimpse of it. I may have said to you before that the world, seen from the Tower, can be drab, even desolating. Such a picture does tend to present itself, I must admit that, but at other times the view can be absolutely splendid. Yesterday, at about three o'clock, I was in my front room – what I think of as both my study and drawing room. I was tinkering with some old equipment that I tend to use as ornament. However . . . all of a sudden I heard the horns. A sharp and rare sound in this quiet spot that has perfected its own unvarying rhythm of birdsong and wind. I rushed to the window and stared out, and in a great headlong burst they broke out of the bracken on the east side, a whole world of intent and earnest animals – dogs and horses and men, and perhaps somewhere pitifully there, a fox. A vision, a vision it was to me: the desperate clamour of hounds and red coats and steaming hunters, baying and sprinting up the runways.

I was delighted by this letter. The one that came on the previous anniversary might have made everything clear, but such a clarification was of benefit merely to us. This latest signalled a new, healthy man in Austin. Writing that account of Vince's death must have been the turning point. It must have been what his return to the Tower, and his skirting round its grim associations, were leading up to. Only when he recounted that story, not just by going over it in his own mind, not just by telling someone in the course of conversation, but by putting it on paper and sending it to the other side of the world, could he put it out of his mind once and for all, and regain his balance. Only by himself officially announcing Vince's death to the family and owning up to his own responsibility for it, could he exorcise that demon of regret and guilt.

'It's been a bloody strange, long road,' I said to my wife as I handed her the letter, 'but he's got there at last.'

She read it, I thought, quite cursorily. 'Poor Austin,' she remarked, 'England has got the better of him at last.'

I couldn't help showing how obtuse and insensitive I thought this was. 'What on earth do you mean? Are we reading the same letter? Doesn't the man's peace of mind cry out to you . . . or whisper to you . . . or whatever the appropriate signal is?'

'Lobotomised, I'd say. Gone off some deep end into a listless, slobbering awe at the pathetic tail-end of old England.'

I gave her the bewildered look that was all my annoyance and incredulity could manage.

'You must admit,' she said, driving home her well-disguised point, 'it was not exactly the holy Lamb of God he saw walking upon his green and pleasant fields.'

'What do you mean?'

'Simply that he's gone into a decline with this second coming and disintegration of poor Vince. I'm not sure that the burden of his guilt . . . no, not the burden of it . . . the baggage of his guilt, didn't keep him tauter, more alive, more imaginative, maybe holier.'

'You're terribly self-indulgent,' I had to say to her. 'For one thing, it's a thousand to one against that he was in any way to blame for Vince's death. And, besides, it's all very well for your romantic notions of the tragic human being, but it's Austin's happiness, my brother's happiness, you're talking about.'

That ended the conversation. She had nothing more to say. And of course, a year later, true to my expectations, there was no letter from Austin. I waved it at her. 'See,' I said.

She waved back. 'See,' she said.

REASONS FOR
GOING INTO
GYNAECOLOGY

She keeps mincing through the room. Her heels, stupidly high for the house, clatter backwards and forwards, spitting out pique and inarticulate frustration and intense dislike. The mood could, of course, be transformed in a moment. But I'm no longer interested in doing so. She goes from bathroom to suitcase to cupboard to suitcase, unnecessary, reduplicated journeys most of them, brandishing her departure in front of me. She hopes, transparently, that I'll stand up, yank her by the wrist as she goes past, tell her to stop the nonsense, and to sit down. But I'm watching porn, fairly soft porn, on the video, and I'm not even tempted to dwell on her pathetic charade. I imagine she looks at the film when she's behind me. She would say it's only curiosity. I would say that's crap. I would say she's a little tramp and would make a sly grab for whatever she can get. But she's cute enough not to let her step falter.

'Instructions for the nappy wash are on your desk,' she says on one of these ghost-train irruptions.

I refuse to acknowledge her. Tomorrow she goes to LA – it would have to be LA of course with her – and straight into the pants of this stud she's picked up.

27

'The cats are due for their operation,' she tries. 'Unless of course you're going to do it yourself.'

I'm impervious. I should get close to six months' peace. As the Puerto Rican rooster loses his appeal, she's likely to discover her maternal instincts again, and head for home. The children will bring her back. Even she knows she's in an exposed position, flouncing out on us like this. Silly, stupid woman, there has never been any prevision in her life, just a flailing around in all the emotional surges that eddy inside her. And when she returns she'll be in no stronger a position: her record of desertion will be against her. Whims all flutter home to roost in the long run.

'Would you mind turning down that nauseating rubbish,' she fires at me.

I let her go through, she disappears briefly, then clatters out again. I throw my arms over the back of the sofa and slide further down.

'If only your colleagues knew . . .' she trails through the exit.

She has a simple-minded view of my colleagues. They're gynaecologists precisely because we all made the same choice at the same age and for much the same reasons. We all plumped for the same option in the full flesh of our virile mid-twenties. Only a complete stranger to commonsense would believe a young man chooses women as his professional concern for purely, frigidly, scientific reasons. 'Your colleagues . . .' she says, and she's never dropped to the plumb obvious fact that my colleagues' libidos have directed their lives in the most palpably comprehensive way possible. Idiot of a woman. If I tried to point this out to her, she would mimic a feeble parody of scorn, reducing my view to sex mania.

The nymphet on the screen is doing her workout and has just bent right forward to touch the ground between her legs and her tights have ridden right up over her cheeks, so far that there's really just a delicate strip of tense material running into her crotch, and it seems it's just waiting to snap and fly open.

'Don't let me delay you,' she says. 'I know you have things to do.'

As a matter of fact, in spite of her stodgily unoriginal irony, I do have things to do. Babysitting's going to be a problem, and I might as well seize this last opportunity. It's all very well having a mother nearby, but there are limits to their usefulness. They can't live with you if you're going to have other women passing through the house, least of all if it's in any sort of volume. We may be great friends, mother and I . . . In fact she's the unassailable contrary evidence whenever I'm told that my relations with women can't be substantial. But there are some things, if known, mother might not find it easy to cope with. There's a limit to what you can expect of another generation. Still, she always sees through the likes of this one soon enough. I'm lucky to have her. In fact a little meditation upon the subject of gynaecologists and their mothers would do all women good. The pattern of intimacy is quite striking. Even more striking is the evolutionary fissure that opens up between the two lines of descent from close bonding between mother and son. On the one side gynaecologists, on the other gays. And, most impressively, the two streams never meet. There are no gay gynaecologists, but within the profession is the greatest concentration of all those qualities that women most admire in the gay sector – the delicate touch, the urbane sophistication, the aesthetic flair, the interest in personality – but without any of the spoiling features, the cruel wit, the unscrupulous gossip, and all the rest of it. The ideal gynaecologist – and it might be surprising how frequently the average comes close to that ideal – is disconcertingly the female cynosure. Not smug. Just true.

The couple on the screen are pretty whacked, but I'm not, so I'll take up the jibing suggestion. 'Don't wait up for me,' I say to her as I pick up the keys from the hall table.

She had the dinner ready when I arrived. She's efficient like that, adaptable, practical. She has a sense of what's needed, and isn't always looking to be treated and wowed. She'll make a good mother.

'Is she really going?' she asks me, once we're halfway down the champagne.

I lean across and brush her fingertips with the fleshy parts of my palms.

All the perfumes on the table mingle. 'Yes, it's all over completely,' I assure her. 'It was long ago.' Then I hasten to add, 'But the door is locking behind her now.'

'I can't have her ghost, much less the shadow of her real physical presence, hovering around,' she says. 'I've had far too much of that.' There is real pleading in her voice.

'I know you have,' I say. My fingers apply just the slightest pressure to her wrist. I've heard all about these half-married men that have insisted on cluttering up her life. I want to reassure her that she's not getting more of the same. 'You must move in as soon as you can. You'll make a wonderful mother to the girls. They'll so desperately need someone just like you. You have so much love to give,' I add. Her face, which has been searching mine, seems to capitulate, and she drops her eyes, and entwines her fingers through mine in mute gratitude. I hesitate to say anything more to her; it wouldn't be sincere or honest. She must make do with what is available to be offered. And she is willing to do that, at least for the moment, and I can feel the responding warmth in that pressure of her hand, and I know she wants me to enfold her, and take her to bed.

It is an emotion, at least the essence of it is, that I see again and again, and my own chemistry responds willy-nilly. There is a feeling of warm, effusive, vulnerable gratitude that wells up in the patient towards the doctor after a gynaecological examination. Just for a start there is the relief that it is all over. The threat of indignity, of violation, has been averted by the sensitive manner, the paternally coaxing murmurs, and the sure touch that is as far removed from the gesture of a liberty as it is from that of distaste. A woman, inspired to feel that she has neither disgusted a man nor been invaded by him, can hardly control the quite hormonal rush of relief that overwhelms her. She is far more vulnerable then than ever she was as she lay exposed on the man's couch. I see the reaction hour after hour, day in day out. I have only ever had one rectal examination myself, and I recognised the reaction at once. I had been more than half expecting it, and, insofar as I had any attention left over from the discomfort of the moment, I had tried to steel myself against it. But the emotion burst out in a way I clearly had no control over. Given the correct handling, women will always respond that way. And there is something immensely satisfying about being the object of the response.

I stand at the bedroom door and dangle my keys. 'Is that young English protegée of yours due back from the country yet?' I ask. I see the tremor of apprehension pass across her eyes. 'If she wants a bit of pocket money while she's here, she might as well do a spot of babysitting. It'd be useful to me.' I watch her tucking the duvet in around the empty spaces beside her, and I know she feels it unwise to protest; she wants to show trust in me, and to be helpful to me at the moment, but, career woman that she imagines herself to be, she is not going to clamour after babysitting duties herself.

'She's due back tomorrow actually, but I'm not sure that she'd really be interested in babysitting. Eighteen going on thirty that she is, I doubt whether she'd be too keen on spending her nights that way.'

'Well, I'll leave it to her,' I acquiesce. 'If she's interested at all. Otherwise . . .' My bleeper goes. I raise my eyebrows very slightly.

'You poor thing,' she says.

I nod, partly in acknowledging agreement, partly in farewell. 'I'll be in touch.'

Dishing out clichés is what the constant practice of most professions is. Clichés to the practitioner, that is. The sensitive man wearies himself with their reiteration. But this profession provides its own best antidote to that hazard. My practice is largely amongst younger women, and they, more than anything else, represent to me the cartwheeling kaleidoscope of life. Unpredictable, direct, autonomous, and quite sharply desirable.

I think of myself as having some style, some finesse, but on this occasion I really did just burst in. The moment she arrived I said, 'Use all the facilities. Make yourself at home. There's a pool downstairs.' She followed the instructions, without any reticence at all, but with that mix of effusive gratitude and giggling coquettishness that seemed to be partly her age, partly the English in her. I was never sure what the message of it all was, and although I took a plunge, I would not, even now, say I got it right. But the risk was worth it.

She kept up, almost to the end, the facade of the child, oscillating to the motions of temptation and reluctance. Hell knows what the rules and the objects of her game were, but she didn't lock the bathroom door, and she didn't immediately and peremptorily order me out. And, let me tell you, she was quite criminally luscious. Ripe and juicy, and with a kick in the tail, or wherever it was, that would leave a snowman howling.

'Could I ask you something?' she says.

I'm running the electric shaver over my chin again before I go out. She's standing in the bedroom doorway, awkwardly, not quite knowing her place. She's playing with the tail of her long straight hair that is held back simply by a rubber band. She shuffles about, and gnaws, in a picking way, at the mane in her hand.

'Of course. Go ahead.'

'It's just that I don't know anyone else out here.'

'Go on. I'd love to help.'

'I think I've got something wrong with me.'

In the mirror I catch her looking up, then dropping her attention again to the hair ends.

'What sort of thing?' Her manner makes me just very mildly uneasy, though I have a perfectly clear conscience. I turn off the shaver, and turn to face her, and give her a light tap of encouragement on the arm. She is not talking about a scratch, I know. More than any other field of medicine, gynaecology involves us with the total human being. An odd paradox that. The whole genital bag of tricks is the machine in the machine – a set of organs that is quite irrelevant to the healthy functioning of that individual. Extraneous really, in the way not even the little toe is. But, touch the sexual organs, and you find yourself responsible for a whole quivering human life. This is real intimacy. In case after case we're sucked into sprawling, often chaotic, personal dramas. And the success of our treatment demands that we intervene and exert control over those dramas. Very humbling.

'I've got an itch I haven't had before,' she says.

'When did you notice it?'

'About a week ago,' she shrugs.

'Just an itch?'

'No . . . it's a bit . . . yukky too. Something's getting onto my knickers.'

'Come on, we better have a look at it.' I hesitate a second. 'I didn't notice anything there before.'

She shrugs again. 'I didn't have my knickers on. And I'd just had a shower.'

I bite my lip. 'You should have told me earlier.'

'You didn't ask me.' And all the time she keeps chewing on her hair, and her face is set with the mild but intractable sullenness of the young adolescent.

The phone rings. There's one beside the bed, but I prefer to take it out in the lounge-room. 'Just sit down there,' I point to the bed. 'I'll be with you in a sec.'

When I return I ask, 'Any chance you could have picked up an infection?'

She pouts and shrugs, and then changes tack and says, loudly and aggressively, ' I suppose so, but I don't see how.'

'Why not?'

'Well, there haven't been many, and I don't see how it could have been any of them.' She waits, and then asks, as much out of interest, I suspect, as of any wish to change the subject, 'Who was that?'

'Your duenna. Just as well she rang before we had the whole of this conversation. She would not have been pleased.'

'What did she want?'

'She just rang to say we wouldn't be going out tonight. She doesn't feel up to it,' I add. I'm given a quick glance, and I'm sure there's something sly, even mocking, in it.

'Well, Miss, why couldn't it have been any of them? All virgins, were they? Cutting a swathe through colonial maidenhood, are you?'

She misses my irony. 'No, not all of them. At least they can't have been.' She was giving a passable impression of being flustered. 'One of them was a gym instructor, and what I mean is that he'd be careful about being healthy and all that.'

I let this pass. 'Where else have you been, Miss?'

'Nowhere really.'

'Well, where not really?'

'Well, just my cousins, but they don't really count.'

'Why on earth not?'

'They're only sixteen and seventeen; they're still at school.'

'But they're your first cousins?'

'But I've only ever met them once before, when we were all little.'

'Where was this?'

'Where was what?'

'How did all this happen?'

'I was staying with them. It was natural. It was fun.'

'What about your uncle and aunt? I mean, where were they? Do you think they would have approved?'

She actually digs her heels into the carpet. 'I came to you for some help. What's all this got to do with it?'

She's wrong, of course. I'm a total kind of person. The notion of holism has always appealed to me. By its nature, my calling allows a complete unity of private and professional life. I'm one of those men of whom it really can be said that their work is their hobby. In this case such a claim could seem crudely adolescent, but my rather more refined meaning should be obvious. I'm a man. Nothing that has anything to do with woman do I find at all alien to myself. I find myself slipping from one role to another as the situation and instinct prompt, until my distinctions become quite fuzzy. I loosen the tie that I no longer need and sit down beside her on the bed.

'I'll give you a scrip for some antibiotics. We'll pick them up when I take you home.'

'Why not tonight?' she asks.

'I mean tonight. You needn't stay, now that I'm not going out. I'll run you home whenever you're ready.'

'I think I'll stay,' she says. 'Actually I need the money, and I don't think I'm expected home.'

Sitting beside her I can't see her expression, but I note the hand again pulling nervously at the ponytail. At least I think there's a nervousness there. I'm determined not to say anything about the money: after all, she's hardly so much as nodded at the kids. And if she hasn't done her job, I don't like the implications of her getting money for other reasons.

'Come on. Up sticks. You'll be happier in your own bed. Besides, I'd like a word with your duenna.'

She stands up, faces me, puts her head on her side, and gives a wry look. 'She doesn't want to see you. I know that. Besides, if I came home early, she'd know something had happened. And I couldn't keep it from her, really I couldn't. She's been such a sweet friend to me since I've been here. You mustn't make me go. Please.' And she twitches, quizzically, at my shirt.

All right. I'll stay put. It's a matter of balance. You have all sorts of patients – wives of prime ministers, actresses, bordello hostesses – and that's simply healthy and sensible. All you don't do is to get them mixed up. Keep the surgery discreet and the waiting rooms separate. They all know they're getting the best from me. And I only charge the common fee.

THE
SAD
MUSIC
OF
MEN

Notes squeaked and bassooed into the air. More bandsmen drew up, stepped out of their cars, buttoning their uniforms, pulling on their caps, trailing horn or cornet or trombone. They assembled on the footpath, between the neon sign that said Nursing Home and the immature eucalypt released from the concrete through one square of earth. They tuned their instruments, exchanged pleasantries, adjusted the small sheets of music, and cast an eye over the loiterers who passed for a crowd. They took the measure of the palisade of brick and lattice, coated in an effusion of jasmine now shrinking and turning brown. They formed ranks, stepping back, some of them, into the gutter, and they hiked their instruments to their mouths. 'Watch' said the bandmaster. Then he raised his baton. The bandsmen took their cue, caught the beat with a nod of their heads, and played.

A tremor went round the walls, and a fissure appeared. Gradually the fissure widened until it eased out a hesitant trickle of patients. Val and Jean and Denis and Glen. Glen held his long, soft face bent forward, too shy to steal more than a glance at the musicians. He clasped his hands across his groin and cringed under the dying jasmine.

'Hello, Glen,' said the middle-aged neighbour. 'Aren't you bringing Doug out?'

'No, no, Barney,' said Glen, smiling, trying hard to explain. 'Not today. Doug's having a lie-down, a lie-down.' Glen's tongue was a swollen slab, without precision, blocking all finesse or definition in the sounds welling from his throat.

Doug's nose is out of joint, thought the middle-aged neighbour. He's the lord of the footpath, and won't mix it with any crowd out here. He has probably deputed Glen who wouldn't otherwise have left him.

'Doug's having a lie-down,' smiled Glen.

The neighbour nodded. Glen had his set speech and all.

The music shrilled and undulated over them. Passing cars slowed and stopped, locals peered self-consciously from their front gates. The sounds of salvation skirled in the Sunday afternoon air, eddied into the vacant lot, clattered around the motley crowd, went racing down the stale-smelling breach into the nursing home, and danced over Doug as he lay in pain.

I'd like to check on them all come together, thought Doug. *See who's out there on the footpath. Barney and Alan and Glen. Barney should be there. He's home on Sundays.* Doug's mind laboured to the top of its next peak. *I don't know about Barney. You can't do much for a weak man.*

Eyes closed, motionless on his bed, Doug caught his breath at the responsibility dropped on him. 'Serve me, Doug,' the Lord had said to him. 'Nothing in the grand style. Just some little harmony. A bagatelle will do. Try Barney for a start. Then whatever else turns up.'

The thought of the assignment exhausted Doug, and he began to pant painfully. He became conscious of the ooze from the side of his mouth. Barney never liked that. Doug could always see him trying to avoid looking at it. And that made Doug wipe it away. So now Doug smudged the viscous discharge between the back of his hand and the pillow. Barney could look back again and not be afraid to face him. He would be able to hold Barney. But not for long. Doug never had long. In the Home he was virtually chained where he was, and when people suddenly came in sight, he lunged out and tried to touch them, but just as quickly they disappeared again. So he waited, spent his days waiting, restrained in the minute circle of his life, till an opportunity was glimpsed, seemed even to offer itself, and then his will lashed every muscle in his being together and he jerked himself out into his mission.

Doug wants a word with me. Pulling his few resources together to manage it. His mouth, in fact his whole body, is lopsided. His mouth has slipped, and slides headlong off the side of his face. Words are squeezed and lurched out in a lubricant of spray and dribble. But his broad shoulders keep him at it. They are outsize so that he has all the elegance of a gridiron player. Those shoulders must weigh him down. He always sags at the knees, but the right leg is bent further than its partner. He forces himself forward, arms stroking, like a man wading through mud. So I go to meet him halfway.

'Hey mate,' says Doug for the second time as he fights his way up the footpath.

'Yes Doug,' I say, 'what is it?' I'm mildly peeved he doesn't use my name. Everybody, male or female, is 'mate' to Doug, but he knows my name is Barney, and has used it once or twice. I dislike being relegated to Doug's undifferentiated mass. I stop and wait for him to reach me. He does, and pauses to catch his breath. He stands close and catches me by the arm, perhaps for support, perhaps for intimacy. His head, and his eyes, not always in unison, dart about trying to see behind me. He seems intent on not missing any car that comes up or down the street. His interest in me seems slight, just someone to waylay. He hasn't yet thought of what banality to produce. Something about the car or the garbage or the neighbour's dog.

'Hey mate,' he says yet again, 'where's your wife?'

Doesn't miss a thing, old Doug. 'She's away,' I tell him, 'just for a few days. Gone to visit her mother.'

Doug doesn't hesitate. 'Who's the other lady?' He doesn't look at me of course. I don't think he does. He's as intent as ever on the cars. I think it better not to laugh, as though I'm in sympathy with a sly male dig. I'm not sure of Doug, how badly retarded he is. He may be quite innocent. He's giving nothing away.

So I play his game. 'That's my sister-in-law, Doug. You know, my wife's sister.'

Doug says nothing. He loosens his grip on my arm and drops his hand as an open truck comes over the rise and bounces, overfast, down the hill. Doug watches its progress intently. 'Might've been Ted or Alan,' he says.

I take advantage of his distraction and turn to my car. 'See you later, Doug. I must go.' I don't think Doug gives me a second glance, but I wave as I ease the car away. 'Bloody Doug,' I say. I'm annoyed.

Doug worries about Barney. But he can't do anything further. The effort is more than he can stand. Trying desperately to hold things together. He feels the strain even through the night, the tight hold across his chest as he tries to bring and clamp things together. And in the morning, when he gets up, more effort. Waiting on the footpath, before first light, while his thigh bones seem to be forcing his ribs together. Waiting for Alan and Ted riding high on their garbage truck. *I don't know that Alan and Ted really like me*, he thinks. *But that doesn't matter. They work with one another, not with me. They flash past me, have a whole life before, and a whole life after.*

But no one else is around even to see that much. No one else can hear the sharp disharmony across the early morning, or can grope, with a blind finger, just for that instant, among the discords. 'Alan today,' says Doug, 'it's Alan's turn.' He grows excited, and his breathing quickens and he strains to listen and to be ready and to keep the pain away.

The truck rolls down the hill, freewheeling in the early morning, no engine, no waking all the residents. Ted uses this hill to roll a new fag. Just one wrist on the wheel, a few toes tapping at the brake. Then he'll exercise his lungs a few times preparatory to roaring the life out of old Doug. Bugger the residents if he can score on that one. Get Doug to give him a nod or wave, and you'd believe he had struck gold. Ted's jealous of me. I can jump down, have a word to Doug as I yank all the lids off, toss the bags and boxes up. So Ted bawls his lungs off all the harder. Simple-minded sort of bastard, our Ted. Needs everyone to be his mate, even old Doug. Sometimes I wonder why I stick on the same truck with him. A wound-up warning of what a man can become: venous face, smoked-out lungs, jellied gut, moribund cock. But he has to prove the world is his friend. 'G'day, Doug,' he bawls. 'How you going, Doug?'

I dance down off the running board, and lope towards the bins. Doug is standing between them and the wall, out of my way. He has his overalls on, the hardwearing industrial variety. They carry marks of yesterday's spaghetti and tomato sauce. Doug has both hands under the shoulder straps. He dislodges them as I approach and takes a step back as though he's somehow wary. 'Morning, Doug,' I say to him quietly, as Ted spits out his salvo of 'G'day, Doug, how you going, Doug?'

Doug doesn't say anything, but his mouth hangs open as I catapult the black plastic bins on to the truck, and receive them back, one-handed, swinging them with one continuous stroke back onto the footpath. Doug moves back in for a closer look as I bend to the cardboard boxes and flick them up, in rapid motion, always at least two in the air at the one time. Doug leans forward, his hands up, fingers tingling like a saint in ecstasy, a long skein of dribble swinging from his lower lip. 'Hey,' he says, and points to a few fragments of paper it is not strictly our duty to collect. But I follow Doug's instruction.

Ted leans across his cabin and bellows, 'Had any naughties this week, Doug, you old stud?' He leans back, congratulating himself with his own laugh.

Doug's head jerks around a bit, his eyes unsure where they can rest safely.

Ted leans back, remembering his punchline. 'Watch them poofters, Doug.' He yanks his thumb in what seems to be my direction. Doug says nothing. His face just screws up a bit. Doug's no fool. The brain mightn't be there, but he's got some kind of sense for what's off – or who's off.

'See you Friday, Doug,' I say to him as I swing back on board. Ted jerks his foot off the brake. We roll forward.

Doug extends his hand as though he's thinking of waving. 'Bye, Ted,' he calls.

'Alan,' I shout at him, 'not Ted.'

'Bye Ted,' he calls.

Doug is exhausted. He looks around, holds out his hand for Glen. But no one is there. His hand shakes and swivels, trying to break out past the pain into a country where the feeling of good health is newborn yet dynamic all at once. 'Glen,' he calls, but the saliva just bubbles at his mouth, and subsides even before it reaches bursting pressure. He gives up the effort, and just waits for Glen. He has done it before, he knows, and Glen came. *Years*, thinks Doug. *I watched out*

*from the balcony for years. Every morning I had to swim out
past all those beds, all those chairs, and wait for someone like me
to come. For years. And then Glen came. Carrying his own
suitcase, so I knew he was the one. He's here, I told myself, I'm
ready to begin.*

Doug has been here since the place opened. So he says. He's
more like me, has an ordinary sort of face, and we're forty
together. The other patients do what he tells them. He tells
Jean not to climb out through the railings on the steps. So she
doesn't, that time. He tells Val not to pull her skirt up when
she's forgotten to put her pants on. So she lets it down again,
slowly. From their sort of faces you can't tell what they think,
but they do what Doug says.

Doug goes outside. He sits on the balcony, but he isn't
pushed there or wheeled there. He comes and goes when he
likes, and keeps an eye on things. And he sits on the steps and
stands on the footpath. He doesn't seem to be afraid of
anything. But he doesn't go to work. I go to work every day.
Over to Rozelle in the bus. And Doug's always there at home
when the bus gets back. Usually he doesn't say anything, but
I think he sometimes looks at me when I get out, and we
always have tea together, and most often I'm still with him for
cocoa at nine o'clock. Then we have breakfast together in the
morning. But Doug doesn't call me Glen, doesn't talk much,
just asks questions, and when you answer, you wouldn't
know if he hears. I don't know what he really likes or wants.
But it's good being with him. You take notice of Doug.

On the weekends we go out together on to the footpath. I
see if there's any boxes or rubbish lying round, and if there is I
put them under our tree. Ted and Alan will take them.
Everyone brings us their rubbish and it always gets taken.
When I've finished that, I say to Doug, 'We'll go for a walk.'
His eyes move around, but I don't know what it means, and

he starts to walk. I walk too fast for him, so I have to wait.

'Hold my hand,' says Doug. He holds it out to me. It shakes a bit, waving from the elbow. I look up the street. There's no one coming. But there's a nurse, Barry, over the balcony. His arms are brown and strong in the short sleeves of his white coat. He's smiling. He might be looking at us.

'C'mon Doug,' I say. 'There's no need. You can do it all yourself.' I'm turning back to him. Waiting. I'm leaning towards him, with my hands behind my back.

The black dog comes out of the house. 'Sandy,' says Doug, and the fingers he holds out move up and down like he's playing the piano, but not very fast. The dog doesn't wag her tail nor look at him. She limps off across the street. Doug looks like he's frowning at her.

'It's Sammy, Doug, not Sandy,' I tell him. 'Come on.' I take a step up the hill, and I half-turn, waiting. Doug begins to lift up his feet again and push his way forward. 'Just to up here. Then it's easy,' I say to him. But he stops again, and rests against a brick fence. He looks around as though he's after something or has some worry. But I'm not sure if it means that. 'We'll go around the block, and then it'll be morning tea time,' I say. But Doug doesn't budge. He looks as if he's catching his breath. Then he gathers himself, and pushes out, but more as if trying to reach me than to walk up the hill. I want to keep on going, but I daren't. To stay a few steps ahead might be the only way of keeping him on the move, but he looks as if he mightn't make it, he looks as if he's asking for help. So I stay still and wait for him. He reaches me and grabs me by the arm, up near the shoulder. He holds on tightly and rests. He doesn't look at me, but I won't try and catch his eye either. Barry has gone in off the balcony, and Sammy, the black dog, is asleep on the opposite footpath, in the sun. Doug starts walking on. I go slowly, to suit him, just like a bridegroom. But as we go, his grip loosens, till I just feel the lightest touch of his fingers above my elbow. He leaves them there as we walk up the hill together. He doesn't stop again or lag behind. Then I realise that I'm not really supporting him, that he doesn't really need me. He's all right by himself. When we get to the top and turn the corner, his fingers lift off and he lets down his arm and keeps walking. But he takes me by the hand. There isn't anything else I can do, so I hold on and keep walking with him.

Till we get home again, and then I have to let Glen go so I can pull myself up the step. Glen stands just behind me. He doesn't touch me, but I know he's there. He's bending and watching to help me. I can't let go of him, I know he's holding me. I'm going up. Not easily, it's a strain, but I'm going up, I'll manage it, and Glen's coming too, hanging on to me, I can feel him. Up we go together. It's an awful strain, but it's not Glen that's the trouble though I know he's there. But the strain is terrible, and not just in my arms. It's sliding in from my armpits, and tightening around all my top and my middle. Is someone trying to pull me back? But Glen's there, and there must be others too. Help me, help me up. Glen, where's your hand, Glen!

They're standing on the footpath, and the walls are gapped. They're idling, or mooching, or taking in the spectacle, or ashamed to be there, or serenading their lungs out. The old black labrador sits staring. As the bandmaster raises his stick at her she thumps her tail on the warm pavement. The mongoloids stand in relief along the wall: Val carries a black handbag over her arm and keeps plucking her skirt down; Jean curls up against the steps, one arm, but no more, laced through the railing; between them Denis has rested his white blindman's stick against his leg, has tilted his police cap to the back of his head, and strums solemnly, and in time, on a toy guitar.

Barney looks at the women, at Val and at Jean, and at the two dark-stockinged, bonneted girls playing cornets. He wonders about them and about their needs, and then about his own needs, and his thoughts slide into a wry grief that Doug is such a nuisance. But he resolves not to be beaten, and so the brass sings to him of love. The litter drops onto the footpath, and the spirits of Alan and Ted hover, joined and disjoined, oscillating between rhythm and disharmony, as they scour for rubbish and consolation. Lost in the jasmine Glen humbles himself, and his hands clasp one another with determination, and his long head drops and jerks and lolls, and no one can tell whether he has his own way of keeping time to the music, or whether he is having a benign fit, or whether he is simply sobbing.

In the centre the bandsmen and the two girls and Denis play on. 'Catch,' they cry as they spray up their barrage of notes. Above them all, riding on the air, catching the notes as they rise and marshalling them into music, dart Charles Wesley and his brother John, Mrs Fanny Crosbie, and the Reverend Isaac Watts, and a dim host beyond number. The nimble, dextrous saints juggle the shrapnel of sound. From the burning gobbets they weave a net, and the net, supple and endlessly elastic, floats out and sinks down, covering and then embracing all the halt and the lame.

PRESS
CONFERENCES
OF
AMBASSADOR
SWEENEY

The story . . . is about this fellow Sweeney that
argued the toss with the clergy and came off
second-best at the wind-up. There was a curse – a
malediction – put down in the book against him.
The upshot is that your man becomes a bloody bird
. . . and could go from here to Carlow in one hop.

Flann O'Brien, *At Swim-Two-Birds*.

Near the end of the third millennium of his crucifixion, Sweeney received a diplomatic posting. Australia, he was told, was ripe for his experience. Sweeney puzzled over the remark. 'Am I to be active or passive?' he asked. 'Who am I,' said his interlocutor, a civil servant, 'to instruct a wise old bird of your . . . perspicacity?'

Sweeney took up his appointment in time for the Bicentenary. He was, said his letters of accreditation, the personal choice of the people of Ireland for the people of Australia on the occasion of this axis in their history.

'How was your flight, sir?' asked the Press.

'Let me tell you now,' said Sweeney. 'Coming down here was the best little hop I've ever had.'

'Why was that, sir?' asked the Press.

'I could see,' said Sweeney. 'I had visions. It must be a great country for visions. It worked me into a right lather, a real frenzy.' Sweeney alternately nodded and shook his head. 'Even I in recent times have found the old passion ebbing away. But, ah, this lifted me. Everywhere I looked there was a

51

revelation. As I surged on, and I don't mind you knowing it, I was a female. There they were, the engines, wobbling like great breasts, proud and powerful and mighty reservoirs of support. Hold hard, Sweeney, I said to myself, you're in for a few surprises in the course of this outing; I was a woman, but no creature of short-winded delicacy. And I looked down and I saw my shadow; only it was not a shadow but a giant fish moving over the water. And the fish proved amphibious, and we sped from the sea across a beach into a continent. And there were bays and lakes that were fine frosting, or fine mesh maybe, and they were so sensitive that the wakes of even the smallest boats endured so long that they settled into the permanency of scars. And almost right here, guarding the city, the wooded Hawkesbury range. It was not mountains, it was not hills. It was massive animals crouching, economically, in a litter, rump to shoulder; which was which there was no distinguishing, but contour fitted contour, and they must have been asleep, though I knew they'd be waking soon. And to tell you the truth I could have alighted amongst them. They were worth praising,' said Sweeney, 'and, to be frank with you, congenial to a man of my disposition.'

'You sound so fresh, sir,' said the Press, 'that I suppose you'll be off now to see the sights?'

'Ah man,' said Sweeney, 'what do you think I've been doing since dawn? Didn't I thunder in over all the backyards, and there the revelations were, burgeoning beside every fence and next to every clothes line. The smouldering tree and the burning bush, jacarandas and flame trees, shrieking to every man, woman and dog that they had a message. I've seen my sights for today.'

'They're all very dull really, Mr Ambassador,' said the Press, 'compared to what we can show you, the Bridge, the Opera House, the Centrepoint Tower . . .'

'Good God, man,' said Sweeney, 'they're a noisy class of

ornament altogether. You're unlikely to extract much good from them.'

'You're quite wrong, sir,' said the Press. 'They're our major money spinners.'

On another occasion the Press gave a cough of token embarrassment before speaking. 'If I may advert to one matter, Mr Ambassador . . . it seems best that you should have the chance to clear the air before people start to mutter behind your back. It's true is it not that you have spent some time in an institution?'

'Ah well now,' said Sweeney, 'not entirely. In fact, not at all. Quite the reverse. The fact of the matter is I spent time in the open air.'

'Isn't that rather playing with words?' said the Press.

'Lord forbid,' said Sweeney.

'I've been told,' said the Press, 'that you were, in a manner, at one time certified.'

'Ah, that now,' said Sweeney much relieved. 'Well of course. Certified by one lad or another here and there. But aren't we all?

'I beg your pardon?' said the Press.

'Well any fellow that's worth a tinkers's cuss would like to be thought mad once or twice in his time. I was mild enough: I took to the woods, I dined on the odd mouthful of watercress, I gave out with the occasional song and manufactured a few quatrains every fortnight or so.'

'That sounds very . . . civilised,' said the Press.

'I was different in my time,' said Sweeney. 'Nowadays I know you've any number of boyos, and the other sort too, dipping their toe in the wild life. But they'd have all the mad frenzy of a telegraph pole. Go mad, or stay at home and eat bread and butter,' concluded Sweeney.

'Take to the trees, you mean?' asked the Press.

'Why not?' said Sweeney. 'Look at the African lad with the diaper and the crocodiles for friends. If you can manage it in the Dark Continent, you can manage it anywhere.'

'Come, Mr Ambassador,' said the Press. 'You don't seriously want us all to live in trees?'

'Now look here,' said Sweeney. 'Tell me now. Do you keep any decent number of lunatics here at all?'

'Well, I couldn't tell you the numbers,' said the Press. 'We keep them under wrappers pretty well.'

Sweeney was appalled. 'Now isn't that the right idiot of a thing to do! Do you not know a blessing when you see one?'

'They could be dangerous,' said the Press.

'Malarkey!' said Sweeney. 'I'm not talking about the odd lad who takes a hatchet to his grandmother.' Sweeney stopped, and looked hard at the Press. 'You do have the common-or-garden species of lunatic, I take it? Even if you don't know how to make use of them.'

'Mr Ambassador,' protested the Press. 'These remarks seem to be going beyond the pale of diplomatic protocol.'

'Stuff and onions,' said Sweeney. 'You need help. We'll arrange a delegation. A few of the fundamentals of the nurture and disposition of the insane in a healthy society.'

The Press had an insight into Sweeney's point. 'Ah, of course, Mr Ambassador. You mean insane only in very much a manner of speaking.'

'Insane is insane,' said Sweeney.

'Of course, Your Excellency. And you'd be interested to know that we do have a lot of people already doing their own thing.'

'I am not,' said Sweeney sharply, 'talking about fashions.'

Another time Sweeney assembled the Press on his own initiative. There was one issue they had never raised with him.

'You're all young fellers, I note. And the odd lass,' he said. 'A word of advice may be useful.'

The Press tittered and looked puzzled.

'Watch the clergy,' said Sweeney. 'They're a diabolical gang of ruffians. Rapacious for a start. I had this slice of land . . .'

'Who are we talking about?' interrupted the Press.

'The clergy,' repeated Sweeney.

'They have a very low profile here, sir,' said the Press.

'Exactly,' said Sweeney, 'You need to watch them like nothing on earth.'

'No sweat, sir,' the Press said, 'they're a harmless bunch, they mean no ill.'

'They'll fleece you, put the evil eye on you, send you to the devil.'

'Not here,' said the Press. 'They wouldn't be allowed. And there's no danger of it in any case. You'd be surprised. You'd never notice them for all the mischief they do.'

'They're responsible for more unhappiness and lunacy than a whole galaxy of moons,' persevered Sweeney. 'I met this madman once . . .'

'Very nice meeting you again, Mr Ambassador,' said the Press. 'Always look forward to our encounters.'

'What is it, Mr Ambassador, now that you've been here for a while, that you feel fits you for this particular posting?'

Sweeney stretched out his legs. 'Well now,' he said, 'I've been a leaper in my time. The long jump, the high jump. That's a specialty down here I believe, in this corner of God's parish.'

The Press wrinkled their brows and their poised pens stuttered above the pads.

'Wasn't it only the other day Ronnie Delaney was telling me about it. Ronnie remembers it well. And why wouldn't he now? Ronnie's big moment and all.'

'He did a lovely sign of the Cross after breasting the tape,' said the Press.

'Ah well now,' said Sweeney and he was embarrassed, 'it was a weak moment, and the priests haven't let him forget it. The priests now . . .' and Sweeney pulled himself upright in his chair. 'Have I ever spoken to you about the priests? They're the . . .'

'What was it, sir, about Ronnie Delaney?' interrupted the Press.

'He shouldn't have won,' said Sweeney. 'He wasn't the best man you know. Ah, I'm sure you do know. There was your own lad, Tandy. And there was that other fellow, the after-hours medical man from the other place. Over there.' Sweeney gestured in an easterly direction.

'Not New Zealand?' said the Press.

'Ah no, not New Zealand,' said Sweeney. 'The other place.'

'You were saying why Delaney shouldn't have won,' said the Press.

'It's no good for the soul,' said Sweeney. 'No offence to Ronnie now. A finer lad there's not. But look at Ireland's soul. A healthy, pulsing class of a thing it is, and why? Ireland doesn't come out on top. Never has. Ah, Ronnie misjudged that one. What can you do with a win? Where can you go from there?' Sweeney leaned forward, keen to get his point across. 'Take the tax imposed on the cerebellum when you don't come out on top. Now don't you stretch and strain for all sorts of excuses . . . and for very good reasons too? You do now, don't you?' Sweeney leaned back, then he leaned forward again, raising his finger.

'Ambassador,' said the Press, 'why do you see us as a nation of leapers?'

'Well now, not every one of you, naturally,' said Sweeney. 'But Ronnie told me of your great moment there in nineteen hundred and fifty six.'

'In the pool?' prompted the Press.

'Ah there's no pool yet at the Olympic Games,' said Sweeney. 'Pool has about it a whiff of the sort of thing them Greek boyos wouldn't have gone for. Alcohol and cigars and horse races on the wireless in the background. It wouldn't be fitting now.'

'What did you, as an outsider, Mr Ambassador, see as our great moment? If it wasn't the pool, was it the track? Betty Cuthbert and the others? Australia's golden girls perhaps?'

'I don't know the Golden girls myself,' said Sweeney. 'We've not many Jewish folk in Ireland. But several from the one family were there? That's a grand achievement now.'

'We'd very much appreciate the Irish idea of Australia's great moment,' persevered the Press.

'It was in the twilight,' said Sweeney.

'There's no twilight here,' said the Press.

'In Melbourne, in the twilight, Ronnie told me. Chilla Porter in Melbourne in the twilight. Coming out of nowhere, and going, I believe, nowhere. Most of the time a most perfunctory sideshow, his event. Jumpers never get their due. A lad may spring into the most almighty leap, and there'll be few enough there to see him and fewer still to praise. And it's sheer poetry, a leap. A lad does it, and he looks back at the leap he's leaped. Did I ever do that? I can't believe it, he says to himself. But it's there, all that ground that he covered in one step, and he can see it. Where was I?' said Sweeney.

'In the twilight,' said the Press.

'Of course. The light fading, fading, and the legendary black man who, they said, had merely to put down his name to pick up his medal, the black man loping around but getting more and more worried as the light faded. And Chilla Porter, the lad from nowhere – saving you gentlemen's pardon – edging up and closing in, jawing up to the bar, holding it there with the promise of a kiss while his legs ran up into the air, and the trunk followed and turned itself, and the shoulders rolled over, and the promise of the kiss held, held, with the lips but a fraction removed from the cold, temperamental bar. Till he was clear. And the head was flicked away and the bar spurned again. Ah, the roars through the twilight. Not a soul gone home. A leaper receiving his dues. The apotheosis of the high-flying man. Chilla Porta in Melbourne in the twilight.'

'Never heard of him,' said the Press.

'Have you not?' said Sweeney. He was stupefied.

'Ah well,' said the Press. 'One more gold in that December . . .'

'Gold me arse,' said Sweeney, 'I never mentioned gold. The lad was beaten soundly. There's no way he'd have won. The darkie had the real rubber in his legs. But, by the Lord Harry, Chilla Porter was your great moment.'

'Never heard of him,' said the Press.

'What will you be doing in your retirement, Mr Ambassador?'

'More of the same,' said Sweeney. 'I've this place down in the country.'

'Live off the fat of the land, eh?'

'If you put it that way.'

'Champagne and steak?'

'Not at all,' said Sweeney. 'I've no palate for that class of victual.'

'What then, Mr Ambassador, is your idea of a good meal?' said the Press, warming to accustomed work.

'Well now,' mused Sweeney, 'I'm very partial to milk.'

'Come now, Mr Sweeney,' joked the Press, 'you're not that old.'

'Indeed I'm not,' agreed Sweeney. 'But I've a weakness for it all the same.'

'Depends how you like it, I suppose, sir,' conceded the Press. 'Could you perhaps tell us something of your preferred recipe or style of presentation? No doubt in your position you'd be able to have some knowledgeable kind of woman prepare it for you. I shouldn't think a woman could refuse you anything,' suggested the Press archly.

'She's a farmer's wife who does for me,' said Sweeney, taking no notice of the prurience. 'I'm a boarder as it were. A very hospitable woman.'

'A mine of wonderful old country recipes, I suppose,' prompted the Press.

'Ah well now, that she may be,' said Sweeney, 'but I've never tried her on that. She fixes me the right mouthful every morning.'

'And how does she serve it, sir?'

'Well, it's after the milking, and the cows have been let out through the yard back into the field. And they make a mess one way and another as they pass through. Now the cowpat in the old country is a different class of product altogether from what you'll find around here. Indeed the name is hardly applicable back home. You tend to get a looser, centrifugal spray of liquid. Whereas here it's one peristaltic wave of the matter plashing into the bullseye of the last, and targeted in its own turn by the next wave. The final product is a mound with a slightly sunken middle, and a series of circular tidal lines. I find it,' said Sweeney, 'one of nature's most imaginative artifacts. The Australian cowpat that is.'

'Excuse me, Your Excellency,' interrupted the Press, 'but you were telling us about your diet.'

'Good heavens, woman,' said Sweeney, 'what possible interest could it be to you what an old Irishman puts in his mouth?'

'You were advertising milk and talking about cows and their output.'

'I was,' said Sweeney. 'And I'll continue to do so. Now if I was retiring to Australia, the cowpat you encourage here would suit me grandly. As it is I make do – and well enough mind you – with what we turn out at home. And occasionally it approximates to the Australian lad. The cow might stand still for a while. Or it might have recently ingested a coagulant, natural or artificial. The pat, as a result, might be firmer. For my purposes these are the ideal. This good woman, the farmer's wife I was telling you about, comes out of the shed behind the cows with a small pail in her hands. She looks about for a pat of some solidity and maturity, but not one that is altogether dried and crumbly. She selects and approaches it. She raises her heel, and, in the manner of the standoff digging his hole at Lansdowne Park, she brings her heel down sharply through the geometric centre of the cowpat and some way into the mud beneath. She shifts forward several inches twisting as she goes. She lifts out her foot and bends over with the pail and pours into the fresh clean cavity its own volume of the warm milk. She's a fine eye and she judges to perfection. Then she calls me, and I go out, and down onto my knees and take my breakfast.' Sweeney's eyes misted over with nostalgia and anticipation.

The Press was silent.

'The good life,' said Sweeney. 'The perfect dish. Raw, fresh, with just the right balance of aromas. Does a man a power of good, and a great way of keeping his head clear.'

The Press was silent.

CAN
THESE
BONES
LIVE?

They drove down the peninsula towards the end of Europe. The road was flat, the land alternately sandy or marshy.

'This is boring,' said the boy.

No one responded.

'Why have we got to come here?' insisted the boy. 'It's just boring.'

His sister, an older child, gave him a look that tried to express both agreement and censure.

The man glanced into his rear-vision mirror. 'We're going to have a look at our beginnings,' he said. 'This is where we sprang from.'

'Yuk,' said the boy.

'I didn't,' said the woman, but very quietly.

The man said nothing, but the grimness with which he looked ahead hardened. The car sped on, careering away from civilisation; the stone walls beside the road were irregular and frequently crumbling.

'Why are we driving so fast?' asked the girl.

The woman said nothing. She turned her head fractionally towards the man, deflecting the question onto him.

He too said nothing. His speed did not alter.

A small green sign, upon them almost before they could read it, said *Ancient Monument*.

'Let's have a look at it,' said the woman.

The man braked and swung the car sharply down the bohreen. They found a graveyard, but nothing else.

'There should be a church,' said the woman.

'Well there's not,' said the man.

'Let's explore,' said the boy. He ran in ahead through a broken gate, just sufficiently ajar to give undisturbed access to dogs. The girl followed more cautiously. Then the woman. She was businesslike, serious about seeing what had to be seen, and about keeping an eye on the children. The man tailed along. He was morose and unwilling.

The woman tried to interest him. 'Not exactly an aesthetic graveyard, is it?' she said.

He looked around. 'It's a mess,' he said. 'More like an abandoned mine than a cemetery.' The vista was of mounds, worn-out, sandy soil, and weeds. 'Not too many graves either, if it comes to that,' he said.

'Was there a war here?' called the boy.

'What do you mean?' replied the woman.

'There are these things like they have in the war,' explained the boy. 'You know, concrete in the ground that they hide in and shoot out of.'

'Pill-boxes,' said the man.

The woman laughed. 'I see what you mean. No, there's never been a war here; those are vaults. We have vaults at home too. But ours are a bit different. They're usually outside the ground.'

'Why do they have them,' asked the boy. 'Why don't they just have proper graves?'

'Well,' said the woman, 'they're for families. If you all want to be buried together.' She gazed at the sand-strewn, elevated blocks of concrete. 'These must be vaults for the poor,' she said, largely to herself. 'The poor Irish families. They all huddle together in death.'

Her husband stood slightly behind her. 'You don't really know all that,' he muttered. 'Don't start giving them some sort of romantic view.'

But the children were off, tearing up and down the mounds, poking and kicking at objects half-hidden in the dry earth. The parents watched from a distance. There was nothing in the landscape that could seize their attention, and draw them, and set up a perspective.

'It's not a normal graveyard, is it,' murmured the woman. 'There is no serenity here. Nothing of the tidiness of rows of headstones. Nothing of the completeness of inscriptions. No sense of lives that have run their course all bedded down together.'

Without saying anything the man moved away a few paces. 'Come on now,' he called to the children, 'that'll do.'

They took no notice. They stood together, on the far side of one of the concrete mounds, quiet and peering at something in front of them. Then the girl broke away and scampered back to the woman. 'Mummy,' she called, 'quick. Come and have a look. It's something awful.'

The woman took the child by the hand and hurried towards where the boy still stood. The man trotted past them and then strode on ahead.

'What are those?' said the boy pointing.

'They're bones,' said the man.

'Yes, I know, but what sort of bones are they?'

'Well,' said the man, 'if you really do want to know, they're a tibia and a fibula.'

'Are they people's?' asked the girl.

'Yes,' said the man.

'What do they have them for?'

'A whole host of reasons,' said the man. 'For arching a bit of leg, for playing footsies under the table . . .'

'They're bones from your leg,' interrupted the woman. 'They're for running and jumping and going up on your points at ballet and stretching out to make the swing go higher and even for just swinging when you're sitting on a high chair. All the sorts of things you do when you're happy.'

'What's this?' asked the boy who had not seemed to be listening. 'It'd make a real good club, wouldn't it?' He bent to pick up the bone.

His mother gave him a sharp warning tap on the arm. 'Don't touch it,' she said.

'Why not?' he asked. 'Has it got germs?'

'It's a thigh,' said the man. 'There's nothing wrong with a thigh.' He jabbed at it with his foot. 'Very succulent objects, thighs. They swivel. They're very good at that. They open and close.'

Both children looked up, puzzled and screwing up their eyes.

'Talk to the children,' said the woman. 'Not to me.' She turned to the boy. 'A thigh is something that enfolds you,' she said. 'You sit on my lap and my thigh holds you there. You snuggle down between my thighs.'

The boy wriggled in some embarrassment. He looked sceptically at the bone in front of him. He turned to the man. 'It's just an old bone, Dad, isn't it?' he asked.

'Just an old bone. And a club. You're right there. Can be a very threatening piece of work. Ah yes.' He gave a reluctant sigh. 'The rule of the thigh.'

The boy continued to look puzzled. 'And what's this one?' he persevered.

The man was starting to lose interest. 'I've no idea,' he said.

'It's a pelvis,' said the woman. 'You sit in the pelvis. All the funny fragile bits of you can rest there.'

'Is it a man or a lady?' asked the girl.

'It's dead,' said the man, but his voice was soft.

'I know,' said the girl, 'but do men and ladies become all the same when they're dead? Or can you still tell?'

The woman crouched down. 'They're never the same. This one is a lady.'

'Really?' said the girl. 'How can you tell?'

'See that corner. That's called the subpubic angle. See how wide this one is. If it was a man it would be much smaller.'

'Why?' asked the boy.

'Oh, I wouldn't like to say,' said the woman, dusting down her fingers and easing herself upright.

The man tried to look through the back of her head.

'Everyone knows the answer to that,' he said to the boy. He spoke with exaggerated concentration. 'Women are more generous, more open, they can accept more, they can take more on. You name it, they can do it. And all because of a right angle in the pelvic bone.'

'Is that true?' said the girl to the woman.

The woman considered for a moment. 'There's a case for it,' she said. 'But you'll have to decide for yourself.'

'Keep an open mind,' said the man. 'Don't take too much notice of what I tell you.'

'Hey,' called the boy. 'Look what I've found.'

The girl ran to him, and peered, and then leaped back. The woman caught her round the shoulders and steadied her, and bent to look herself. 'Isn't that terrible,' she said as she eased back, 'allowing the place to get into that state.'

'It's a real skeleton,' called the boy to his father who had remained at a distance.

The girl gave a wary, side-on look down the wide tunnel that led into the oversize burrow. 'It looks like a dead sheep,' she said. 'Why does it have all those round things?'

'To keep in the heart,' said the woman. 'Look at it. It is just like a cage, isn't it? The heart will disintegrate long before the cage will open its bars or fall apart.'

'What do you mean?' asked the girl.

The man came up with them. 'Let me interpret the oracle,' he said. 'The ribs keep everything in place. If they weren't there, your heart would be running into your lungs, or your heart and your lungs would be diving into your stomach. Which means that just because you were panting you would think it was your heart at work, or just because you were hungry you could say it was your heart, and so on. I merely give one or two examples.'

Both children looked again at the skeleton. The woman made no comment.

'There are more of them there,' said the boy probing the darkness. 'Lots of them.'

The girl walked away to one of the other mounds. She stood at the entrance and put her hands on her hips, and gave a bold look into the darkness. Then she walked on again and repeated the action at another entrance. The boy, irresolutely, watched her.

'They're everywhere,' she called back. She bent over from the waist, hands still on her hips, and screwed up her face against the contents of the tomb. 'Look at these ones,' she called.

The others all obeyed her.

She pointed. 'Why haven't those two got any hands?' she asked.

The woman answered, but in a tired, quiet manner as though she were speaking to herself. 'So they can't touch one another,' she said.

'Why not?' asked the girl.

'It would be dangerous if they were able to touch one another. Those bony hands are very sharp. They can do all sorts of damage. And they're so cold and hard. Imagine if you saw a pair of hands like that, moving towards you to touch you and then to hold on to you. No, it's best if there's no hands.'

'No,' said the boy. 'No one's frightened of a skeleton's hands.' He gave the woman an exasperated look. 'All skeletons should have hands. Where have their hands gone to?'

In the background the man laughed. 'See how close together they are, those two,' he said. 'They were fighting as they went down into the grave. They just opened their jaws and snapped one another's hands off.'

Both children stared into the hole. 'They haven't got any heads though,' said the girl.

'What?' said the man, play-acting puzzlement. 'They have to have heads to be able to bite and spit and poke faces and all the other nasty things skeletons like doing.'

'But they haven't got any,' repeated the girl.

'Before the hands got quite gobbled up, they tore the heads off,' said the woman.

'Yuk,' said the boy.

The woman shrugged. 'But the heads probably weren't worth keeping by then,' she suggested.

WEDDING
PRESENTS
FOR
BREAKFAST

I acquired my mother-in-law by accident. But that's another story. The present point is that just recently I lost her.

The day after this epic turn of events I sat, unshaven, spooning breakfast into my jaded system. My wife sat opposite. We had disposed of certain issues with early-morning dispassion – hours of sleep tallied, milkman's bills, other items of that moment. The flow had dried up. The atmosphere was desultory. I had not thought of the deceased for quite some hours. My wife seemed relaxed and guileless; her chin was retracted. (My wife's chin could dispose of many a stronger man than I.) Then, cool as you please, half in the act of getting up and turning her back to me, she said, 'Mother never opened her wedding presents.'

The coffee being poured into my mouth ceased all vital motion. It simply sat there, a still pool, stagnant. My wife continued to affect the pose of one who has just emitted a supreme inconsequentiality. My mind took off at an alarming rate – for that hour of the morning. My mother-in-law had not married recently. My wife was in fact the fruit of her one and only union. Indeed, years had elapsed between conjunction and this recent, final disjunction.

Gravity proved overwhelming, and the coffee seeped slowly away, leaving my mouth free. 'I heard correctly?' I enquired.

'What?' said my wife.

She was playing with me, I saw. 'Your late mother's supreme act of retention.' I needed the slight tinge of combativeness to draw my wife into the open.

'I understand it,' she said.

'You!' I exclaimed. The remark sorted oddly with my wife. She is an acquisitive woman, much given to a role as a receiver of supplies of manchester, silverware, household items, etc. I looked at her suspiciously.

Never one to share my more personal pleasures, she was making herself a cup of tea. She still had her back to me. 'If you use your imagination it makes complete sense,' she reprimanded me.

'Hang on,' I said. 'Did you ever ask her why she hadn't opened them?'

'Of course. She said there was no need. She had the Hardy Brothers list.'

'And you really thought that explained it?'

'Of course not.' She actually turned round and faced me. 'As I said, you just have to use your imagination.'

'My imagination was never able to contain your mother. My scope was far too puny and limited.'

With even, exaggerated enunciation my wife said, 'It was a statement to Dad.' Then she turned away and actually walked out of the room.

'Saying what?' I called after her, but she ignored me.

Unaided, I applied myself to the puzzle. The statement, if statement it was, could only have been of ill-intent. Yet, to my perhaps naive eye, the old lady had displayed only average hostility towards her spouse. Given her normal outlook on the world, she was almost remarkable in her temperateness.

Hence, I deduced, the statement, although undoubtedly malevolent, was subtly so. Once I had seen that much, the rest was easy. The statement had been a warning. My mother-in-law's commitment to the marital state had always been qualified and conditional. Legally, and perhaps by other imperatives, she had been forced to the ultimate validation of sexual union. But as long as the wedding presents remained unopened, the match remained unconsummated. Neither husband nor wife could touch those very singular gifts traditionally given exclusively to married couples for their mutual enjoyment. The presents remained strictly, *qua* presents, intact, virgin – boxed, wrapped, carded. They were as ripe for return to Hardy Brothers or sender as for defloration by my now late in-laws.

My admiration for the old woman was momentarily, but quite effusively, purged of all begrudging elements. She had produced a warning of quite splendid ominousness.

My wife returned to the kitchen. She looked brisk. Continued conversation with me was not on her mind. But I was proud of my insight; I wanted her to know I had cracked her code. I shook my head in tribute and said, 'The old lady certainly had style.'

'Don't be ridiculous,' said my wife, turning sharply. 'She never had the slightest sense of dress or decoration. Or taste at all for that matter.'

My marriage is like that. Overbearing obtuseness. I try to duck and let it pass. 'I mean I can't imagine a smarter way of letting the old man know there was an annulment round every next corner.'

'You can be so absurd,' spat my wife, and this time the jaw was planted firmly down the wicket. 'It was a very happy marriage.'

Facts are for flying in the face of. For some people. Reason, abuse, are both impotent. Just let the irrationality come, and use it as a source of wonder. Man's jaded experience constantly needs new stimuli. Viewed in this mature, sophisticated way, my wife's howlers can be a most fertile source of gaping and amazement. 'So what was the great statement saying?' I tried to be sweetly teachable.

'Some people!' grieved my wife. Then, with a largesse of maternal condescension, she explained to me. 'She was totally dependent on him. That's what she was saying. She wanted it known he was to be the sole supplier of her needs. Other people's presents would have been just a reminder that she'd taken favours from outsiders. He was her husband. He had to work through the Hardy Brothers list and supply her with everything himself.' My wife bent her head slightly and gave me that quizzical look meaning 'Do you understand now, dear?', and then her expression shot back into neutral before passing immediately into a simper. 'It was all rather sweet, really,' she said.

That was a rebuke of course. Need I say I was not the least bit convinced. My wife's charming romance was a complete fantasy – totally unlikely – deriving in no way from the actual characters whose lives it was embroidering. I made no attempt to make my wife see this stark logic. She is not open to reason. The adventure of my life consists of adapting myself to her unshakeable fatuities. And indeed, from one point of view, it means there's never a dull moment. Some right contortions I have to perform to keep our two-planet galaxy from disintegrating.

I retrieved a slice of toast, spread margarine evenly and to the edges, and wondered whether the palate demanded honey or vegemite. No need was crying out. I divided the slice, and made one sweet, the other savoury. It was difficult to choose which I should eat first. Upstairs my wife made noises indicative of a return to the environs of my company. I seized the honeyed slice, and tended rather to bolt it, racing against the drips that oozed over the rim on every side.

'Chaos,' said my wife, bursting through the door. 'That's all this place ever is.'

Carefully I dusted a few crumbs from my fingers onto the plate. 'I'm finished,' I reassured her. Her flurried manner, in fact, was misleading. There was no crisis or urgency about. It was all merely a statement – in this case to me. 'Actually,' I said, 'I wouldn't mind a word with you.'

My wife opened the fridge. 'I'm listening,' she said. And I knew she was too. Our marital life demands that when I want her attention, I go through the paces of making an appointment. To keep the ploy effective, I use it sparingly. She feigns indifference, but I know she listens.

'I don't want to get philosophical,' I began, 'but, on the question of the presents, where are they now?'

My wife rarely lets up. 'Now, how on earth is that philosophical?' she asked.

I waved this red herring away. 'Just that my imagination seems to be in gear at the moment, and the phenomenon of the presents raises all sorts of questions.'

'I don't see . . .' she began, but thought better of pursuing that line. 'The presents are safe,' she said.

I took the bull by the horns. 'What are we going to do with them?'

'Do with them? Nothing! And what's we got to do with it? The presents are no business of yours.'

This was all so much bluster and smokescreen. My wife in fact sat down, and although her chin was forward there was an unmistakeable foxiness about her. 'The presents,' she said, 'stay where they belong.'

'Which is with us, surely,' I said. 'You're the sole heir. They don't belong anywhere else.'

'Don't you have any feeling for the dead?' She was quite scathing. 'Can't you try and attune yourself to their spirit?'

This was a new tack for my wife, a plain woman at all times. Black was black and purple was purple, and pity help anyone who dealt in pastels. The dead only existed insofar as they were of use to the living. Sensitivity to their tunes was a new line for her altogether. I wondered what was going on. By this time I had finished breakfast, and I believe I was reasonably alert. 'Well,' I tried, 'what does her spirit communicate about her wedding presents?'

'My, oh my,' riposted my wife, 'what's happened to the little man with all his fanciful notions and flowery talk? The old lady's gesture should hit you in the eye.'

'I'm still too affected by her death,' I said. 'Please just tell me about the presents.'

'She's never opened them. She wouldn't want them opened now. She'll have to take them with her.'

'But she can't take them with her. That's usually the point.'

'Spare me your wit! The presents are to be buried with her.'

For a lingering moment my wife intended to repeat her trick of leaving the table on her big line. But the temptation to keep a ringside seat for my reaction was too great.

I saw all that happening even as her latest absurdity landed at my feet. 'For the love of Mike,' I cried, 'have you got religion or something? She's not Pharaoh or his wife or any other Egyptian for that matter. If she didn't need those things in this life, she's hardly likely to need them on her journey to the next.'

My wife remained unperturbed by this outburst. 'If you weren't at the mercy of your own wordspinning,' she said, 'you'd see it was the only possible thing to do with them.' She paused, and then added, 'Unless, of course, avarice is allowed into it.'

She thought she'd stymied me on that one. But I was too outraged to fall for cute attempts at cowing me. 'Avarice has nothing to do with it, and well you know it. Self-indulgent quirkiness, that's all this plan is. And there's no way I'm going to allow it to end up in such wastefulness.' A cogent thought occurred to me. 'In any case, they won't all fit in the grave.'

'I've bought two plots,' she said. 'There'll be two coffins. I'll put some things in with her, some in the box next to her.'

I actually stood up. 'This is your own mother you're talking about.'

'Pooh, pooh,' she said. 'I've never noticed you display such concern for my family before. The old lady will be delighted to be lapped about by her presents.'

'Well, I'm going to take them off her. She had quite long enough to have a good go of them. It's someone else's turn now.' I felt I had put the moral point quite squarely.

My wife resorted to legalisms – a sure sign she was on the defensive. 'Interfering with graves is a criminal offence.'

'I'll plead overwhelming grief. One last look and embrace. Hamlet wasn't charged. And I'm a relative. They'll have to believe me.' I let the challenge sink in.

'You throw all those presents down there, and the moment the last mourner leaves the graveside I start digging.'

'No you don't,' said my wife, and this time she did stand up, and she pushed her chair back in. 'I've hired two guards. They'll be there till the earth settles and the slab goes on. Hang the expense. It's only your money.'

I find it unaccountable that marriages are so commonly regarded as dull, inevitably dull. My wife and I have no difficulty in giving one another constant stimulation. As the worthy woman turned her back on me, I felt every tingling hormone rushing to aid the genesis of my next move. Indeed there must have been a superfluity, for I was yanked roughly down a new alley of approach. 'Hey,' I called out. 'How do I know you really will put those presents in the coffins?' I'm sure I heard a step falter in the front room. 'For that matter,

how do I know there still are presents in those boxes?' There
was silence. Ha, ha, I smiled. Got her on the run.

EDGING AROUND THE FAT MAN

I'm not perverse, whatever the appearances. Ingenious is the accurate word. A bachelor now for many years, I've had a fight to maintain that status. The women have given me a torrid time, but none more so, I might say, than my own sister. A man's enemies shall be those of his own household. Very true, very true. It's enough to make a religious man of me.

I am the stable member of the family. My sister is not adverse to movement. She roams about, in and out of company, and when it suits her she roosts on me. I'm uncomfortable with this arrangement. All of the burdens, none of the pleasures, as they say. She has no kitchen sense, no love of horticulture, no assets. She approximates to the slatternly type.

On this last return she has let fall clues that she is thinking of an extended stay. She has moved my best plastic chair to a shady niche on the verandah and covered it with a piece of tartan material, very worn, of her own. She spends much of the day at this vantage point. Inside she has effected a similar redistribution. But – and it is a subtle move – she is acclimatising herself to my taste in television.

83

She has envinced considerable interest in that pacemaker among football commentators, Rex Mossop.

'He's spoken for,' I tell her.

She sucks her lower lip, and regards the screen with, I have to confess, a salacious leer. 'He may not be happy,' she retorts. 'Men in public life seldom are.'

My sister keeps a scrapbook on such matters. I'm not sure whether her rambles have ever brought her up against any of these items in her scrapbook. Her sojourn with me, I believe, is to provide a look-out on the masculine parade. She wishes to do a thorough refurbishing of this personal encyclopedia. So she watches television.

'Who are them pansies?' she says. Rex Mossop has momentarily disappeared. She shifts one buttock and narrows her eyes at me.

She seems to need a few words on the basics of the game. 'They're the footballers,' I explain. 'That's their dressing room. They're getting dressed. They're Rex Mossop's whole *raison d'être*.'

'Don't you like those bodies?' I ask her. She's fond of a bit of dirty talk.

'There's no personality to them. Do we get a look at that other fellow again?'

'He flashes on and off.' I smile discreetly at myself.

The sister, who is older after all, snorts. 'No wonder you're the way you are,' she says. 'Get out of the way, kids,' she shouts at the screen. Mossop reappears. She is quiet for a moment. Her pupils dilate. She shakes her index finger towards him. 'Now that's what a woman likes – hard, fast-talking, strong, uneven eyebrows emphasising all the points. It tells you there are brains there.' She hangs on Mossop's every word.

I see out the game but my mind is elsewhere. Point one, she is settling in. Point two, she is after a man. Point three, the style of man she is showing a preference for is unobtainable. Point four, she will be settling in for a long stay.

Which is undesirable.

I am still turning this over next morning as we sit on the verandah. The sister has been to the newsagent to scrounge as many issues of *Rugby League Week* as might still be available. She leafs through them hurriedly. It is clear she is not finding much of what she wants.

Looking towards the horizon for inspiration I spy an acquaintance labouring up the street. The person in question, a male, is only an acquaintance. Under this aspect he is an asset. He is a talking point, a name to drop. People are proud even to have seen him. They would regard it, and with every reason, as a nightmare to experience any deeper intimacy with him. As other persons are studies in flair or in nattiness or flamboyance, this individual is a study in grossness.

I observe his approach till he falls within the sister's line of vision. Then I watch her keenly. She registers astonishment, she gapes, then she turns her face away and emits one of those *uhff* sounds that signify 'This cream is off!' or 'It's all over my shoe!'

This breath of disgust is like Newton's apple: it delivers the solution into my head. 'G'day, Onslow,' I call. 'A bit torrid on it, eh?' It is in fact a pleasantly warm morning.

With the back of his hand Onslow curls back the wave of perspiration that is coursing down his brow. Then he slings it over our fence onto the grateful grass. Onslow grunts.

'Have a rest, have a drink,' I say, rising and insisting. He is, I know, merely on his way to the corner shop. He is incapable of ever going any further. I haul him in the gate, sit him in my own chair. I introduce the sister, then ask her if she'd be so good as to get us a pot of tea. Onslow and I exchange confidences on the street, the dogs, the gutters, the weeds, the rubbish. Onslow, I suspect, approves of most of these features. Very probably he contributes to them. I am pleasant, but try to avoid looking at him.

The sister serves us, then returns inside. I hear the television go on. Once Onslow has creaked into the standing position again, been escorted out the gate, and resumed his expedition to the corner shop, I idle in to the sister. 'Nice chap, Onslow, don't you think?'

The sister comes straight to the point. My brain wriggles with satisfaction. 'Calls here often, does he?' she asks.

'On and off, quite a bit, one way and another.' I give an impression of pausing to reflect on my luck. 'A very decent sort of chap. And interesting!'

Her restraint breaks down. 'The only interesting thing about him I noticed was his indecency! Is that all he ever wears?'

She has a point. Onslow confines himself to a pair of shorts. He has never been seen wearing anything more. He does not appear in colder weather; I imagine he stays in bed. 'It's a condition he has,' I explain. 'Very sensitive skin. Can't bear anything close to it.'

'No, that's why he slaps his disgusting bare feet down over every revolting surface. You never bring him inside, I hope.'

I tantalise her by avoiding this one.

'That fat all over the furniture!' Her voice drops, and her eyes widen. 'Do you know that . . . thing hangs so far down that I couldn't even see the front of his trousers!'

'Why do you want to see the front of his trousers?'

'Let me tell you, young man, that in spite of your dearest deluded wishes, we women find trouser fronts excruciatingly boring.'

I back off strategically. This is not my point after all. 'Actually you'd be interested,' I say in a sincere kind of way, 'Onslow does party tricks with that belly of his. You ought to look at it closely some time. It's not just a protuberance. It's a complete new fold to the body. You need to go almost the whole way round his back to see where it begins. When he's had a few, he picks it up by the sides and flaps it as though he's shaking a rug. He always gets a few laughs.'

'You have him here to perform these perversions?' she asks.

'Yes,' I tell her. 'Quite frequently. He's the resident house artist in a way.' There, I think, she'll be off to pack her bags in no time. I want to hasten the move. 'They're great nights,' I add. 'Everyone gets shickered, and we have a great time.'

'How often does this happen?'

'Now and again. We don't plan anything. It just happens.' Keep her guessing, I think. Make her feel anarchy is likely to break out around her anytime.

She gives me a tight, malevolent look. 'I told Mum you should have been strapped more, like us old ones was.'

Next morning she's still with me. She's out on the verandah uncommonly early. I can see she's on edge. She sits there for six hours, doesn't budge – meals, calls of nature, anything. I shuffle around. I'm careful not to offer to get her anything. I don't want any feelings of gratitude or warmth at this stage, much less any suspicion that she's going to be cocooned or spoiled in this residence. I have a few words on the phone to a man I know about the Singleton dogs. I come back outside. Onslow is just coming through the gate. The sister is standing up, hands in an expectant clasp. She sits Onslow down in my chair, and says, 'Be so good as to get a cup of tea for Mr Onslow and myself.'

I'm too flabbergasted to interfere. For one thing I want to tell her Onslow has never had a title in his life. I get the tea, but deliberately only pour enough milk for one cup each. The sister seems to be doing all the talking, although in a subdued, confidential voice. Periodically Onslow distends his belly and accompanies it with a grunt. Thick-lensed glasses and shaggy hair hide any more specific reactions.

The moment he's gone, I tackle her. 'What was all that about?'

'You've just been using that poor man for one of your own vile purposes!'

I feel badly caught out. I had no idea she could be so acute. 'Come off it,' I try. 'I really thought you'd enjoy meeting Onslow.'

'Indeed I have,' she says, 'but that's neither here nor there. And you're just a born liar. Always were.'

I can't see what she's getting at.

'Now you sit down there a moment,' she wags her finger at me.

I subside into my own chair.

'Mr Onslow has no interest in your parties. Do you think he likes his belly? Do you think he's happy with it? Why do you think he plays with it for you and your obscene friends?'

After each question I shrug and try to open my mouth. As I have never held parties and as Onslow, to the best of my knowledge, has never played with his belly for himself, or for anyone else, I am stumped.

'It's what happens to women. The only way they can find favour is by demeaning and humiliating themselves. They're accepted, but only for a moment, and with contempt. Then they loathe themselves all the more. That's how poor Mr Onslow feels. No wonder he hardly dares show himself.'

'Hardly dares show himself!' I gasp. 'The man's a thorough-going flasher, parading all that flesh around.'

'There you go. You have no respect for him. And yet you're willing to make use of him.'

'Oh,' I try and dismiss it all. 'Onslow's happy. Fat people always are.'

'So why do you think he lives with the cockroaches in that

sordid boarding house? Why do you think all his meals are dim sims, hamburgers and coca cola?'

'Because he likes all that.'

'Well the truth is he doesn't.'

I can hardly see why she is so sure of that. To the best of my observation Onslow had not confided one word to her in the whole of their little drink together. 'Rein your imagination in, woman,' I say. 'He has to live within his means. Social security: invalid pension, I should think. And he makes do with that. And he's happy enough with it.' And on my last words I raise my voice and leave the verandah. I have heard the barrier fall at Rosehill.

When I come to review progress on the removal I realise that she's using Onslow as a stick to beat me. But, next day, just as I'm about to peruse some remarks of Bert Lillye on a topic presently close to my heart, she comments, ever so casually, 'Mr Onslow must have a certain amount behind him.'

I put down my paper. 'Why on earth? Anything but, I should think.'

'His expenses are so meagre. Car, fares, clothes, none of those things. It's quite admirable really. Primitive man, without any of those needs the rest of us accumulate.'

'Admirable! Did I hear correctly? Two days ago when you first set eyes on him you almost puked. And once I'd introduced you, you could hardly back off quickly enough. Heaven help us, you women are perfidious! Recoiling with distaste from this, that or the other poor man, or saying how you don't find him at all attractive, or how this type doesn't do anything for you, and lo and behold we turn our backs, and you're hanging on his arm, sick with love and desire.'

'I'm not sick with love and desire, you impertinent little boy,' says the sister, and she rises up halfway out of her chair. 'Your credentials to preach on the subject of women are nonexistent, and, in any case,' she subsides back, 'we were not talking about women at all, merely about Mr Onslow's assets.'

'Well,' I say, accepting this rebuke, 'what do his assets have to do with anything?'

She shakes her head. 'You've got a very unimaginative mind. Given that his assets are what they are and that the man is clearly in need of help and friendship, and here we are with all this room and so much in common with him, it seems only sensible that he should come here.' Her hand makes a few revolutions, signifying inexorable logic.

I stare at her. The revolutions falter just slightly. 'You want Onslow here?'

'Stop suggesting "want" all the time, will you! I think it would be a good idea all round if we took Mr Onslow in.'

I see her meaning quite clearly of course, but I have to make noises to give myself time. However strong the chance might be of Onslow dying prematurely due to the great strain on his heart, and of the sister being the beneficiary of these alleged hoards, I am not going to come at cohabitation with the monster. Let her try and move him, and I move him right back where he belongs. I flex my wits for the struggle. I decide on a frontal assault.

'Onslow has no interest in marriage. He's not that sort.'

'Who mentioned marriage? He can be as free as he likes.'

'Not in my house he can't. We won't have any concubinage here. Our parents would never forgive me if I turned my place over to a house of sin for their daughter.'

'Cut the crap,' she says. 'You and your furtiveness. Don't think I haven't noticed what you've got stuffed away down in the laundry under all those old newspapers.'

'A previous tenant, a previous tenant,' I mutter. I must deflect attention back to where it belongs. 'What I meant,' I say through long-suffering, clenched teeth, 'is that Onslow has no interest in the physical passions. He mentioned that one night when he was rather jarred. Something to do with his weight. Pressure on the pituitary gland. Stops messages being passed from the brain to the lumbar area. You know, he sees an objectively erotic sight, but the burst of adrenalin gets suffocated, wiped out, even before it really starts off. Something like that,' I sum up.

'Fat men are just as lecherous as the rest of them,' growls my sister. 'The rest of *you*.'

'Not Onslow,' I assure her. 'He's as placid as a baby. Hasn't had . . . an erotic movement since he was twenty-one. Day time, night time. Never.'

'He's very charming,' says the sister.

'True enough.' I tell her, though I can't see it myself. 'And if charm's all you want, you're okay. But some people require a bit more.'

The sister does not immediately respond. I can see she's in some doubt. I seize the opening. 'I think your best bet would be to make a clean break now before you get any further involved. Go away for a while. You could only get hurt with Onslow. I've noticed an insensitivity about him.' I can see she takes in the good sense of what I say. She broods.

At last, with resignation, she speaks. 'You never listen. You never have. You haven't given half an ear to what I've been saying, and off you go making up some story. Your waking hours are one story after another for all I know.'

I look at her with resentful hurt.

'As far as I'm concerned,' she continues, 'the subjects of neither marriage nor licentiousness have ever for the least moment been under discussion. Mr Onslow passes on a simple desire to share this house, I tell you, and bugger me if I'm not being knocked over by an epic of lust and dispossesion.'

'Well,' I cavil, 'I wouldn't let him throw his weight around.'

'Listen to me, will you,' she screams. 'There's never been any suggestion of his throwing his weight around.'

'He does it frequently, in a manner of speaking,' I have to remind her.

'He never has in front of me.'

'Of course not. I told you he was respectable. It would be like lifting up his lap-lap.'

'What's the point of being so obtuse, to say nothing of vulgar? You're an impossible man to talk to, to say nothing of having to live with.'

I feel a sharp quiver of hope.

'I wouldn't do it if I couldn't see a better future ahead. It would balance things out if we had someone not a member of the family here. And think of all we could do with Mr Onslow's backing.' She waved her hand around the newspapers, the ashtrays, and my old grandmother's anti-macassars. 'He could work wonders!'

A sound like flippers splats its way across the verandah. A massive shadow looms in the glass of the front door.

'I'll let him in,' says the sister. I peer to see how many suitcases he's bringing. I descry none. And he seems undressed as usual.

The sister talks cups of tea, what a pleasure, the place being a mess, putting some make-up on if she'd known, what a pleasure, draughty on the door step, what a pleasure. And much more.

Onslow's jaw hangs open. He seems at his last gasp. But he's just being normal.

The sister pauses in order to step back.

Onslow speaks. He is economical with words. 'I'm leavin',' he proclaims. 'Just came to say . . .' He appears to run out of words, energy – everything. He withdraws his left hand from its picking at his navel, and jerks it, minimally, just twice. The gesture is not expressive.

'See you,' I say over my shoulder, 'good luck.' I'm not having him in the place.

Nor does the sister insist. Onslow splats off.

Strange, I think. What's that woman up to? 'Well,' I say to her, 'what was all that about? I thought you'd be upset.' She isn't.

'Mr Onslow and I were just working things out.'

'Working what out? He never got a word in.'

'There are plenty of ways of getting a message across that you're not a wake-up to,' she says.

'Look,' I say, 'what is the position? What is Onslow up to?'

'Stop being so literal-minded. You can't pin Mr Onslow down. He's a dancer, he's a magician, he's a free spirit. We have an understanding. Some people could never rise to that.' The sister looks at the ceiling.

I get up and move out to a small private room.

IN
THE
HOUSE
OF THE
DEAD

'There was nothing more anyone could do,' she tells me in the hallway. 'Least of all you or I.'

That's a presumption, I think. She knows damn all about me and any potential I have for doing more. Superficial woman, I conclude. She has to meet someone, it's a crisis, yet she prepares her formulae, and trots them out, with no thought of first feeling out this stranger.

Yet there is delicacy enough in the way she indicates an Australian connection. Two prints from Gould's *Birds* hang framed on either side of the front door. I wonder if they had been a present from our common husband, Arthur. I suspect not. Neither his income nor his inclination had ever run to that extreme of expenditure. And it would not show much tact towards her second husband to leave gifts displayed so prominently. No, it was probably her own acquisition after her divorce from Arthur. Bought with her own plentiful resources. For her own reasons. The two Goulds are not flashy birds. I don't immediately recognise them, and it is not the moment for close inspection and lingering over zoological Latin. Their appearance would not, I imagine, have distracted the second husband. I associate him with money in some form, and possibly for that reason, and possibly because after Arthur any woman would be looking for an uncomplicated rest, I also think of him as an English booby. He would have found a few discreet birds tasteful enough, and accepted her word that they were an investment. So she's kept some kind of faith with Arthur.

I'd refused to go with him. It was the shock he needed, I had decided. I made it clear that unless he did something about himself, it was all over. If he wanted a nurse, he could pay for one. I had not signed on for that. If he came back in the same state I would not be there. Brutally clichéd, but I had no option.

The outcome was less straightforward. It first took the shape of an international phone call. She said who she was, and then launched into a preamble in that sprightly English upper-class way that is considered suitable for all occasions, even the quite lugubrious. Which this one rather was. 'I don't quite know the ins and outs of your marriage,' she said, 'but I'm sure you'd want to be told.' So I was told. Arthur had cancer. The prognosis was totally bleak. It was a matter of weeks rather than months.

'Where is he?' I asked.

'I thought it best if I took him home,' she answered.

'Well, I don't know the ins and outs of your divorce, but that really seems very good of you.'

There was a pause, more protracted than usual at the other end of the line. If I had found her loud brightness a little odd, she seemed to have reciprocated by having doubts about any touch of levity. It was not that I was unaffected by the news. Far from it. I was at the start of a confusion which could only get worse. And, in this instance, I was intrigued, saddened, and yes, even amused by this reappearance of the Lady

Melanie at the centre of Arthur's life. I could never get over the pretty-pretty staginess of the woman's name. 'I presume you met her in Quality Street,' I had once remarked to him. Here she was, stepping forward to attend on Arthur at no doubt his most sordid. In the best traditions of Miss Nightingale, I supposed.

'Of course I'll come straight away,' I assured her.

'We gave him the spare room,' she explains to me over tea. She imagines some gesture of bewildered gratitude on my part and says, 'No, it was the least we could do.'

'Your husband was certainly very understanding.'

'Oh, Bobbo wouldn't mind. He never notices a thing. I could pick my nose at the dinner table and he'd say, "What a jolly nice little something you've got for us, Melanie." ' She laughs more loudly than is necessary between just two people.

Keep your voice down, I think. Arthur's in the house. Somewhere. He doesn't want to be embarrassed by your choice of men.

'Just as well really,' she continues without lowering her voice, 'that he went off so easily. Before you arrived. Things would have been so complicated otherwise. What could you have said to him really? No time for you two to talk about your marriage when he was in that state. But you couldn't very well ignore it, could you?'

I shrug. 'We had developed an understanding.'

'Oh,' says Melanie. 'I'd thought things were more or less at an end.'

Whatever her hospitality, I think, she's not moving in on my marital intimacies. I feel a distinct block against any gush of sisterly sympathy. 'No, far from it,' I say. 'We'd come to an understanding.'

Melanie crosses her legs and tucks them hard back against

the sofa. 'How lucky you were. We never could, that was our trouble.'

'But he was glad to come here.'

'Well of course.'

She seems to be missing not just the nuances of what I say. And, interesting as the prospect is, I haven't really come to make her acquaintance. 'When are they coming to . . . when will he be leaving here?' I ask.

'Not till Monday. It's frightful isn't it? But, you know, London nowadays . . . that appalling fellow Livingstone in the Council, and all his creatures everywhere. You can't even die and be buried in dignity now.'

'I should go up and see him,' I say.

For once she picks up the suggestion in my words, and rises reluctantly herself. 'It has been so nice talking to you.' Then she pauses, and a vision of slight awkwardness quite clearly passes before her eyes. 'Actually,' and she half laughs, 'he's not up, he's down. We couldn't really leave him in the guest bedroom. Not . . . oh well, you know. Things do become awkward. Visitors, and people blundering in, and so forth. It's that fellow Livingstone's fault of course.'

She precedes me out of her drawing room, opens a door discreetly set into the panelling under the stairs, and stands back. 'The cellar is the most sensible part of the house. I've left the light on. I know you'd like to be alone.'

The only appropriate man I know in London bounces down the stairs, just ahead of the voice of Melanie offering instructions and invitations. An academic and a priest, and at least an acquaintance of Arthur, he is in England on sabbatical. I don't know him well myself. I still address him as Father. He, if anyone, is the man for this particular need. So I call him.

A priest, on professional business, should not arrive feet first. Least of all if the legs are stubby and unsure. But as his business is in the cellar, he does arrive that way. So it becomes a matter largely of etiquette. I stand up. A bentwood chair has been placed at Arthur's elbow, and I imagine that the correct way for me to keep vigil is to sit there. It has crossed my mind that the Lady Melanie, having put it there, knows it is the correct way. I am willing to accept her instinct as to *comme il faut*. I stand up out of deference to a priest. Does his entry take precedence over the focal importance of the dead? I call the priest Father Jim, a gesture that balances professional acknowledgement with grateful friendliness. He kisses me. It's on the cheek, but it's a kiss. He stands back, giving his glasses a slight shake by the frame, the picture of concern. What next? I can't talk to him about the death, not least because I hadn't been there. And I haven't summoned him because I feel like conversation. I make a slight gesture of my hand towards Arthur. The priest should do with the dead what he has to. That is all I have called him for. He should attend upon Arthur according to his lights, as an accompaniment and relief to my own vigil. His profession, I take it, is to gauge the requirements of the moment and to introduce whatever grace he can into even the most inauspicious and graceless of occasions. Normally, and as one less wise, I would have expected some Latin recitative and some douches of Holy Water. But from an academic, and presumably a modern, I am not sure.

I sit down again. The priest shows little interest in Arthur's face. He blesses himself, and I even feel a shiver that the gesture is done in the old superstitious way to ward off evil, rather than to mark the opening of a ritual.

'We'll kneel down,' he says, 'and say the Lord's Prayer.'

We kneel and he prays. Arthur lies just above eye level. It makes me feel he is disdainful.

'We'll pray silently now,' says the priest. 'Let us remember Arthur, and let us recall the ... stimulation and ...

enjoyment he gave to so many people.' He pauses, obviously thinking hard, but not, I think, quite hard enough. 'Let us thank God, the loving Father of all men, for the presence of Arthur amongst us, and let us commend him in all his lawful frailty to that same loving and all-merciful Father.' The priest is silent and his eyes are closed but his hands move ceaselessly from a prayerful clasp to an optician's twitch at his glasses. The gesture distracts me. He makes it portentous. It is an adjustment to the purposeful cascade of molecules through his brain. I stare at this mechanism for prayer.

The remembrance and commendation of Arthur require two minutes. Then, on cue, I stand again, rubbing the grit and the white bloodlessness from my unprotected knees. The priest keeps his head bowed, and I imagine we are to go through the same routine in a number of different poses. I prefer to be seated and informal while I remember Arthur. But I also prefer to do so in the company of the living when the alternative is a weekend of solitude.

The priest does a little act of pulling himself out of a trance. He does it well – just the discreetest suggestion of vestments being shrugged off, and the wrench at having to tear himself away from the company of God. But I am ready for his company now, and for whatever initiatives he might suggest for keeping our unchosen vigil.

Then he turns to me, clapping his hands together very softly, and at once I can see the gears changing. 'I should know this,' he says, 'but what is the name of Lady Melanie's present husband? What form of address does he prefer?'

I glance at Arthur. His own sense of decorum had never been unerring, but this confusion would have been totally foreign to him. I must half-expect him to rear up in indigna-tion. I certainly feel apologetic towards him. 'Freddie,' I tell the priest, anxious to hurdle this embarrassment quickly and cleanly. 'She is "Lady" entirely in her own right. Her father was or is the something of something. Freddie's nobody. As it were.'

'All I need to know,' says the priest. 'You're too good.' He takes half a pace back, and once more twitches at his glasses. 'You're a marvellous woman. So wonderfully resourceful.' He thinks about kissing me again, but instead he says, 'I'll be offering Mass for you both in the morning,' and up the ladder he goes. The voices break out like bubbles as he reaches the top.

I sit and try to recall the presence amongst us of God's servant, Arthur. But as a preliminary, only one thought comes. 'Freddie' is not the man's name. I have no idea what it is.

Arthur had had me to come home to. That was the trouble. By late afternoon he could be helpless. He didn't need any evening hours to write himself off. Home he would blunder, and I would be there to clean him up. The task didn't even call for extended hours. My life wasn't disarranged by him. I believe he actually thought like that. Shock, and reliance solely on his own resources – that was the only way I could see, if he were to pull himself out of it. I suppose I got the first shock, but it was savage enough to have an elastic effect. One of his colleagues told me. A story out of the archaic epic about the poet Chris Brennan fouling his room at Sydney University, but this version had suitably modern touches. Arthur was vomiting the contents of his morning and lunch-time drinking, and any bits of food he hadn't been able to avoid, into the drawers of his filing cabinet. After that he'd decide, not unreasonably, that he was sick. He'd close the drawer, and go home.

I sit here, at Arthur's elbow, periodically glancing at the face, wondering what I can do, but my imagination is pinioned by that disgusting filing cabinet. Perhaps it should have been a sign to me at the time when it was a daily event, but the gross realism of the gesture overbore its symbolic value.

Arthur's life had not been without achievement. His professional life, that is. Though the signs look bad I wouldn't presume to speak for the rest of it. He was an authority in his field; he was asked to speak; he'd had his notable publications; some students had looked on him as a real mentor. But he'd ended up vomiting into his filing cabinet. A soundly contemporary gesture. An update of Aquinas, after his vision of heaven, saying of his vast theological opus, 'It is as straw'. Except that Arthur never had a vision of heaven. Not even, if I may be facetious, in my arms. And my arms have been disengaged, for a long time now, long before the filing cabinet started to get the thumbs-down. I am sure Arthur would not have received any other entrées to paradise. It is much more likely he'd been having visions of hell. Moving into an eschatological phase at any rate.

Come on, I tell myself, this dispassionate, ironic tone is not appropriate. A turmoil of emotion is what's called for. Other people, not you, can sit in their little pools of calm. And from upstairs, the pure essence of voices – male, Australian and ingratiating; female, English and braying – are filtered down to me. That's why you have been left here, I tell myself, in tactful and discreet solitude. You didn't accompany him on his dying. Your proffering of support, and your grief, have been telescoped into these few hours. Lord alone knows what zany shapes they might take. Your emotions could tear you apart.

I steal a glance at Arthur, uneasy that even in his blotto state he'll catch me out in my tearlessness. He looks dignified. Most men with any facial bones do look dignified in death. Hidalgos every one of them. Nothing in life became him like the leaving it. But he appears not to notice anything. Or he doesn't mind my dispassion. He looks noble, there's no doubt of it, and he's giving nothing away.

I wonder what's going on behind the death mask. Does he want me to be here? Does he perhaps mind my being here? I feel a sudden emotional leak. We hadn't written, we hadn't been in touch at all after he'd left home. I'd seen him out the door, bowed by my threat. I'd watched him shamble off, a pilgrim determined on his miracle. But perhaps I'd got it wrong. Or perhaps he'd had a conversion all right, but it hadn't been towards me. After all, he hadn't asked me to come over.

I stand and bend over Arthur's face. The capillaries have all drained. The alcohol is no longer disfiguring him. The long-entrenched flush has gone. He is pale and in control. No longer the soiled and sordid late-afternoon figure. The nose and lips rear at me in pride. I lean over further and, at first tentatively and then merely gently, I prise open the jaws and sniff. Arthur's breath is not sour. I can never remember it so.

Above us I hear the high-pitched scrape and tinkle of heavy silverware on fine china, and all the sounds that issue from the cavities of human beings. They are more unrestrained, they are coarser all the time. Tunelessly chairs scrape and are knocked, shoes shuffle and click about in nervous betrayal.

'Quiet,' I ask them, but in a voice I hardly hear myself. 'It's disgusting isn't it,' I say to Arthur. 'No. That's entirely the wrong word. Pathetic perhaps. But only we can see it. All the untidiness and artificiality of the strings and levers that make the puppets work. The chemical kitchen as people spark together. All the wastage and irrelevance of action in the push towards an instant of compatibility or, more rarely, joy. We see it from the ideal vantage point, Arthur. Very few get to stand here.' I lean over and kiss him on the forehead, a laughing playful nuzzle.

The braying and the ingratiating are losing their identities as the volume increases. The poise goes out of individual voices and they merge. On the floorboards the shuffling, the tapping, the squeaking become less tentative. Feet beat time rapidly, they move into a gallop, they falter, and chairs jar and scrape, and the feet sprint on again, and silverware echoes no longer against just the chinaware, but against the crystal and the thick wood of the table.

'Come on, Arthur,' I call to him. 'We have more to jangle about than any fortuitous collocation of mummers.'

My voice grows bolder. I step back from the catafalque and swing the bentwood chair away. I kick off my shoes so that they spin up onto the floorboards above us. 'Come on, Arthur,' I repeat. 'The occasion calls for nothing less than a rhumba. Come down, Arthur. Arthur, come down.' My heels arch and fall, and above me my shoes clatter rhythmically across the floorboards. Arthur is swept up, he is carried away. He tells me he was desperate to be beside me again, that my ultimatum was all he needed, that I could not have done more for him. He shouts this at me, almost hysterically, above the thudding of the dance band. I pull him close and whisper that the cruelty of it tore me apart, that I have never wanted him more than I do now.

All the irrelevant cacophony fades. The band, the dance floor exist solely for us. But we don't need them. I turn out the lights, I lead Arthur across the room. Into the soft, expansive bed I pull him down beside me. 'Kiss me,' I tell him. I let my lips open towards him, and in the sweet odour of reconciliation I swoon.

THE
LIFE OF
A MAN'S
MAN

Once, when my satisfactions were less subtle, I spent an afternoon at Wimbledon in bed with a Polish lawyer. But all flesh is grass, and the rains came and the winds blew, and on my next visit to Wimbledon there was no trace of the pearl-pale, elusive Polish body. And anyway, this time I was there from a higher motive.

Lovers, I thought, and no doubt marriages, come and go, but the love of two good men endures, if not forever, well at least across a host of more carnal, and quite stupid unions.

Michael had made this appeal with some finesse. I had not been thoughtlessly summoned: a passer-by yanked in to hold the dike as soon as the first sign of trouble appeared. Nor was it a case of my being any port in a storm, or the scrapings of the barrel to meet the crisis. 'I've been thinking,' Michael said, 'you are the right person. I know you've got a lot to do, but I'd be very grateful if you could see your way to helping me out just this evening. I tried the clergy. I got on to the Jesuits down there, but they prevaricated as only they can. I had to give a complete medical history, and submit to a mini-dose of the Spiritual Exercises, before they'd consider setting foot outside the door. The fact of the matter was I could hear the television in the background.'

So I answered the call, taking a mild satisfaction from stepping into the breach that the clergy had abandoned. The world had been scoured by earlier rain, I had had a surfeit of my own company for the day, and I rather looked forward to this glimpse of life in the raw.

The flat was upstairs, through two puny pineboard doors. Not a habitation for the spirit, I decided. The smells of old fat and stale cigarettes hung together, viscous, in the air. I was introduced to a kitchen and a bathroom, chilly, linoed rooms both of them, installed in the 1920s, with enough dust and detritus and disregard for hygiene about them to inhibit any urge I might otherwise have felt to touch and use and make myself at home. I was shown into the lounge-room, or more properly the work-room, or more accurately the pit or the ring. It was so dreary, so dun. The rust-closed windows framed dust, the sun-bleached, cheap furniture, a grey carpet worn and dirtied, walls bare except for the nail holes and adhesive remnants of former tenants, the anaemic brown tables and low bookcases scattered with manuscripts and scores and books, all covered, in some perverse dedication to drabness, in brown paper. Who would do that to an adult's books? I wondered. But the mood was in keeping with the atmosphere. Recreating the foul rag-and-bone shop, I thought. There was no radio, a portable record player that must have come onto the market about 1955, and a small piano. The lid was down, and piled high with paper, printed and unprinted, and with used crockery and ashtrays. In the middle of the room, on all fours, was the man of the hour, the composer.

The etiquette books don't envisage the half of it. How do you greet in this situation a man you have met several times, with whom you are on automatically assumed first-name

terms, with whom you have talked solicitously, even intimately, about a common friend, and who you know has a
need to dislike you that is restrained only by self-interest? I
did nothing.

My host took over. 'We have a visitor, Edward,' he
announced. He spoke with the rising inflection that does
duty for the aged and infirm.

The composer had his head on the floor, resting in his
hands. He moved it very slowly from side to side. His pose
gave nothing away. Is this an act? I wondered. Or does the
position give him relief from an aching head or a fiery belly or
whatever other physical blight several bottles of vodka had
caused? The rarity and unnaturalness of the pose made it
impossible to interpret. I just stood there, trying to take my
cue from Michael, trying to avoid certain airs, readying myself
to adopt others. I must not, I warned myself, appear
patronising or contemptuous; I must be prepared to be
tender, or to defend myself.

With a gentle gasp the composer collapsed his hips, and
rolled over into a foetal position. In keeping with the pose,
the fingers of his left hand moved, like a baby's, in a
tremulous clawing motion. Although his eyes were open I
could not help watching his face. With agonising slowness
his mouth was trying to form an O, a passage for the tongue.
But the mouth was quite dry, completely without lubrication,
and the tongue was a miniature staggering drunk itself, so
that it could make no headway to wherever it would like to
have gone. There was just a flaky rustle and the popping of air
against the roof of the mouth.

Michael knelt down. I thought he was remarkably forbear-
ing, even gentle. 'Come on, Edward,' he said, 'what about
sitting up. You'll be much more comfortable.'

Somehow, by one of the lurches of his tongue or quavers of
his fingers, the composer must have signalled he preferred his

place on the floor. Michael just patted him on the shoulder
and stood up. Clearly I was not going to be greeted or
acknowledged, at least not in any of the more orthodox
fashions.

We went out to the kitchen. 'It's very sad,' I said, 'to see
him reduced to that.' And I knew that I was also quite pleased
to have encountered the composer in such a state. I would
never feel any need now to be awed or diffident in front of
him in his more creative or exalted moments. And he was
displaying what he was capable of, what he was really like, to
Michael, and the lesson could only be a salutary one. Oh yes,
the sight was sad, but not without its saving graces.

Michael looked at me, and I felt he was measuring the
sincerity of my last statement. But he must have decided in
my favour. 'It'll do him good to see you,' he said. 'He likes
you, you know.'

Three weeks before, when I had arrived in England, the
symptoms were already breaking out. Within hours of my
landing Michael had rung me. It was obvious he was distracted. After what I suppose he judged a decent interval, he
broke off to ask me if I'd have a word to Edward who, he
claimed, was dying to speak to me. The false note grated, but
of course I said yes. So the composer came on, and I could tell
that Michael had left the room. The composer was quite
drunk – a fact that Michael had not even hinted at. He
delivered what I must call a fulsome address. 'It will be so
good for Michael to have you over here,' he said. 'He's very
fond of you, you know,' and there was a pause in which I was
to insert an acknowledgement and some reciprocation. I
suppose I did so. 'He's been thinking about your arrival for a
long time. I believe you should know it's been worrying him.
He's desperate for your approval, you know. He just fears you
mightn't approve of his love for me. And it's a wonderful
love, you know, a wonderful thing.'

You right bastard, I thought. What transparent bloody tactics. I didn't have to say anything. The drink was moving him along with great fluency. I just absorbed his various jabs, and consciously steeled myself to face in the exact direction he was trying to dissuade me from. I had not known Michael had decided on that sexual preference; I had certainly not suspected he had chosen to express it towards this object. But if I was suddenly enlightened I was certainly not surprised. The only shock was in recognising this blatant attempt to poison me. It had never occurred to me I could be seen as a rival to another man. Much less that my affection for my purported beloved would have to be killed off in this manner.

The world, in its perverse way, tasted quite sweet when I put down the receiver. A quarter of an hour before, I had nothing against the composer, and even after this conversation my reservations – no, my objections – had little, that I could see, to do with my personal interest. But the composer had revealed himself as a pretty noxious helpmate for anyone, and especially for someone to whom I wished well. But I knew, when I finished on the phone, that the man even produced the very rope with which he was going to hang himself. I felt, not so much satisfaction, as relief that there would be no need for me to take an active hand.

Later, during the dark, I said, 'He seems rather docile.'

'No mood can be relied on to last,' replied Michael. 'It's the range and the unpredictability of them that wear you out.'

I knew it was probably premature, and possibly counter-productive, to say my piece, but the opportunity was too tempting to pass up. So I said, 'Why do you put up with it then?'

Michael shrugged, but more, I suspect, as a reflex than as an expression of any real ignorance. He certainly didn't delay in responding. 'I know it must be hard for an outsider like you to appreciate, but you do a lot for genius. And he is a genius, you know. At least, if that word has any meaning at all, he's the nearest embodiment of it I've ever come across. And you don't sacrifice genius unless you really have to.'

It was no good disputing whether the composer rated the title of genius or not. I knew the ranking he was given in the latest edition of *Grove*; I knew that among the more advanced critics and musical theorists he was judged as nothing more than an old-time melodist of mediocre charm. But I could make no personal assessment; I was no musicologist. And, in any case, it would hardly be tactful to dispute the man's ability.

'Do you really think genius is worth all that? I suppose I'm of the old school,' I said, 'but the whole Romantic idea of the artist is just a licence for all kinds of blood-sucking and self-indulgence. Once you subscribe to it you're giving your artist a green light to treat you as ruthlessly as he likes. You've got no comeback.'

Michael stood up and went over to the stove. 'Except that it doesn't work like that. Not in practice. Would you like some soup?' He took a large, uncovered bowl from the fridge and up-ended the contents into a saucepan. 'Pea soup,' he said. 'It'll be nice and warming and filling.'

Who made it? I wondered. How long's it been there? We stood, in silence, till the soup began to simmer. The composer stumbled out onto the landing, and eyed us. 'Old times?' he said. The articulation was laboured and this reinforced the sardonic tone.

'Would you like some soup, Edward?' said Michael.

The composer faltered forward into the kitchen. We both stood back – to avoid, I think, being further obstacles to his progress. He made his way to the stove and peered into the saucepan. 'Shit,' he said. 'Do you expect me to swallow this shit! He lifted the saucepan and tipped the soup slowly onto the floor. Michael lunged at him. The composer threw the saucepan across the room. 'Don't insult me with that shit!' he shouted, and he left the room.

The chill light was beginning to press through the uncurtained windows.

'At least he hasn't started another bottle,' said Michael.

I could not feel impressed. 'Presumably there isn't one *to* start.'

'That means nothing,' said Michael. 'He just orders me to go and buy one.'

'Why on earth do you take any notice of him?'

I really could not tell whether Michael's look was shamefaced or whether he was trying to suggest my callousness and stupidity. 'He makes threats,' he said, 'and I see no reason why I shouldn't take them seriously. You don't call the bluff of someone in that manic state. Or at least I wouldn't.' He paused. 'Why? Do you think I should?'

I was saved from an answer by the appearance of the composer. 'Would our guest,' he said to Michael, 'like to hear some music?'

Michael interpreted this as a positive mood that had to be encouraged. 'I'm sure he would,' he said. 'What did you have in mind?'

'Don't bother,' said the composer, turning his back again. 'He's musically illiterate.' His voice was surprisingly controlled and sharp. Michael did not look at me. I saw no point in disputing the jibe. An accident of birth, as it were. And anyway, I work on the premise that you don't get into arguments with a drunk.

The composer fell heavily into an armchair. 'Put on those Copland suites,' he ordered.

Michael did so. He came back, and we stood in the kitchen, out of the way, till the record caught on a crack, and stayed there for minutes. Michael returned to the lounge-room. I tailed after him. Suddenly he leapt, screaming, at the chair. A mess of spent matches lay on the carpet. The composer still had a lit one in his hand. He was extending it towards the pile of manuscript on the table beside him. His quavering hand was trying to coax the corners and overlaps of paper to accept the small flame. Singe marks darkened the tiers of manuscripts. Seeing there was no inferno to fall on, I stood and watched.

'I need the matches,' said the composer, 'to light my cigarettes.'

Michael was irresolute. 'Tell me when you want one, and I'll light it for you,' he offered.

I saw the flaw in this safeguard. I felt no inhibition in pointing it out then and there. 'A cigarette is even more effective for incendiary purposes,' I said.

Michael put the matches in his pocket. 'If you can't be trusted,' he said, 'we won't leave you by yourself.' Aaron Copland played on. We sat in the two angles at the base of the triangle and watched the apex.

'Jackals,' said the composer. 'Talentless little parasites.'

Michael went out for food. The composer rose from his chair.

'Where are you going?' I asked him.

'To bed,' he replied. 'The only place where I can get any peace. You won't follow me there will you.'

I didn't feel up to any repartee with him. I ignored the arch invitation.

He felt compelled to follow it up. 'Of course you're petrified at what you might find out about yourself there.' He felt his way, still unsteady, out of the room. 'Keep that music going,' he called back. He slammed the bedroom door after him. I relaxed and picked up the poems of Betjeman. As far as I could see it was that or the works of Mary Wilson.

'Music,' he shouted through the wall. The Copland suite started for the umpteenth time. *What strenuous singles we played after tea,/We in the tournament – you against me*, sang the Subaltern in my lightened mind.

When Michael arrived, in the aura of chips and cooked chicken, I jumped up and restarted the endless music.

'Where is he?' asked Michael.

'Gone to bed.'

'Has he? That's most unlike him.'

'Well, he's in the bedroom at any rate.'

Michael tried the door. It opened, but hardly more than an inch. We both pushed hard. It gave slowly till there was the crash of an opposite reaction. 'Open up, Edward,' Michael called. We pushed harder, two marginally fit younger men against a middle-aged drunk and his bed. We burst in. The composer fell back onto the bed. The suggestion of smoke and smoulder lurked in every corner of the room. A radiator, glowing, lay upended in the furthest corner of the room. Lumps and wisps of kapok had been pushed through the guard onto the glowing bars or left festooning the grille. A slashed pillow lay beside it, and larger clouds of kapok had found their way across to Michael's bed where they had all expired, but not before leaving heavy burn marks on the sheets and blankets. The composer hoisted himself from his bed and came at us. I let Michael lay hands on him first; it seemed the correct thing to do. Then I stepped in and helped, and we wrestled him away from the radiator.

'Sit there,' said Michael, 'and stop this childishness. If you want to be trusted you'll have to show you can be.'

'If you want to be trusted . . .' repeated the composer, and he rolled back on to the bed. 'If you want to be trusted . . .' and I could see that behind the stumbling mimicry there was his own brand of the mocking laugh. 'Ah, but do we want to be trusted?'

'Let's have something to eat,' said Michael. 'We'll have it in here.'

I sat on Michael's bed, a tissue draping my shoulder, and on my knees chips and part of a chicken carcass. I lifted a chip and began to eat.

'What's this disgusting crap?' asked the composer, coming towards me to peer at the plate.

I looked down. 'It's perfectly respectable,' I said.

'It's crap,' he repeated.

The plate was whisked from my knees. With an accession of agility that was miraculous he danced to the window, flipped it open and flung the plate into the night.

'Hey!' came a first cry of expostulation from outside. A gate clicked. There was a hubbub of voices.

He slammed the window. 'We don't bring that crap in here.' Then he relapsed into his shambling helplessness and staggered back to his bed.

For an instant I felt like applauding, and then like laughing. Finally I came to what should, normally, have been my initial reaction. 'I've had this,' I said to Michael. 'Poison the man will you. Put him down, put him to sleep somehow.'

'I'll have that drink now,' announced the composer. He lay on his back and intoned his wishes to the ceiling.

'Give it to him,' I said, 'he can't get any worse. The faster he can race towards oblivion the better as far as I'm concerned.'

'He's been here before,' Michael explained to the intern, a woman, a girl; she would have been no more than twenty-five.

'He's not an alcoholic,' Michael explained. 'He does drink a lot, but only at times of great tension.'

'What does he do?' asked the intern.

'He's a composer,' said Michael. 'A very well-known one.'

'Excuse me,' I interrupted, 'do you really need me here?'

'You might as well stay,' said Michael, and the intern acceded to this with a distant nod.

'So,' continued Michael, 'he works under great pressure. Just at the moment he's writing a Mass. For Our Lady. There's a deadline. The conductor for the first performance is supposed to have the *Kyrie* and the *Gloria* by the end of next week. It's a very difficult piece, the *Gloria* and the choir . . .'

'Yes,' said the intern. 'So it's pressure of work really?' The relief was visible.

'Not entirely,' said Michael. 'It came to a head the night before last. I have this friend, a common friend really. He and I had to go somewhere together.'

I found myself frowning. My chronology of the last few days was, by now, quite confused. Michael didn't look at me at all.

'Edward was working very hard, but he was in bed by the time I got home. The next morning he discovered a love-bite on my neck.'

I looked at the intern, but almost surreptitiously. Her expression was blank. Her head was poised. But it was poised in that prodding way, wishing him to go on so that she could win time to find an angle of approach. I wanted to tell her how embarrassed I was that she was being put through all this unnecessary detail. But maybe the farce of the passions of these middle-aged men was not registering with her. She looked a child of innocence enough. Or maybe she was actually relishing it all, fighting to keep the blank, professional air in place. Most of all, I think, I wanted to disown these strange men I had arrived with, I wanted to tell her I was not the friend mixed up with love-bites, that I was not indifferent to her, that I was on the side of women, of the angels.

Michael was embroidering on. 'Edward said hardly anything. Just that I was a slut. Then he went out. And came back with the bottles. Do you want to know the details of his drinking then?'

'No,' said the intern. 'It's not necessary.'

'He winds down on Guinness. He has had treatment for this trouble in the past, and the doctor looking after him has approved the Guinness as a good braking measure.'

'We don't allow any alcohol in Outpatients here,' said the intern.

'No,' said Michael, 'I didn't mean that. I think you'll find he's had a surfeit. But I know at this stage he needs professional attention.'

I looked at Michael. What he meant was that he himself needed a few days' rest and sleep. The hospital was a child-care centre for him. Edward's alcoholic history was too good for them to refuse him admittance. Michael would not catch my eye. 'Doctor's got everything under control,' I said to him. 'A film wouldn't go astray for us.' I tried not to sound as though I were extending an invitation, making a date. But he'd hang around all night unless he were given an alternative, and an order.

For a moment he was hesitant. The intern looked from one to the other of us with her same blank patient look, as though waiting for the family to tidy up their little domestic problems. 'I'll just say goodbye,' he said, 'and tell him we'll be back in the morning.'

I didn't bother disputing his assumption. I let him go, hoping I might have a chance for a private word with the intern. But she accompanied him.

'He'd like a word with you,' said Michael when he came back. 'He really would.'

He lay on the trolley, behind curtains, dressed already in the white hospital gown under a white sheet. In his right hand, clamped to his breast, he clutched a crucifix, in his left a phial of what I knew to be Lourdes water. There were tears in his eyes.

'Come here,' he said, and he opened out the arm that held the Lourdes water. 'Closer. I want to kiss you. Please let me kiss you.'

I had no alternative. I leaned in. The crook of his arm, a blunt instrument for love, closed behind my neck. Steady, I told myself as I converged towards the stubble and the dry, open, malodorous mouth; it wouldn't do to baulk. I won't have him accusing me later of open revulsion. But still, there was no obligation on me to be the active partner. I kept my mouth closed and eyes open, and my face landed in the clean white crook of his shoulder. I could feel his lips moving about my ear, with what meaning I was not sure, although I had no doubt he himself knew exactly what he was doing.

He sobbed. Or it sounded and felt like a sob. 'You can't realise,' he said, 'what a cross this talent is. I didn't ask for it. It's crippling, crippling. And you can't get rid of it. God asks me to pay a fearful price for His gift.' And I could feel his knuckles and the agonised contours of the crucifix pressing into my chest.

You calculating bastard, I thought. Every inebriated step you take you know exactly what you're doing. How can you get so drunk and yet keep your wits so sharply attuned to your own self-interest?

'Love is the only thing that keeps me going,' he whimpered.

I gritted my teeth. I couldn't even feel embarrassed for him. Just totally cold. Is that the emotional standard of your art? I wondered.

'I love him,' he said. 'I really do. And it's the only time he ever has been loved.' The elbow loosened around my neck. I knew that he wanted to see my face. I ignored the hint. He took his arm right away, and forced up against my chest with the crucifix. 'No one's ever really loved him before, have they?'

I was standing above him. 'I don't see much evidence that he's really loved now,' I said. 'When he's not a doormat he's a nursemaid.' I couldn't bring myself to add, 'Or the object of unwanted and bilious lechery.' For one thing I might, in spite of what I was told, have been wrong. No use allowing the man an out.

'He's loved,' the man repeated.

'No wife would call it love. Not nowadays. Not even in the worst-regulated marriages.'

'Oh . . . Oh fuck you,' he said in a dispirited tone, rolling his head from side to side. But then he thought better of it. He raised the crucifix to his lips and kissed the Christ figure. He adopted a sad tone. 'You don't know what love is,' and he jiggled the crucifix up and down as if to suggest that I was excluded from the community of understanding that he and Christ shared. 'You've never loved him. You just took him or left him. I can't do without him. He's never experienced that before.'

I forbore making the obvious comment. 'Well, just show it,' I said in what I intended to be a mild, even compassionate voice. I gestured at the placebos he was clutching. 'And ditch this gimcrackery. You're just bringing religion into disrepute.' I must have felt a surge of proprietary chagrin. I would have preferred medical staff not to be treated to this display of infantile piety from a plastered, abusive queen, brought in after a domestic over love-bites.

By way of answer he kissed the crucifix. 'Don't you understand anything?' he laboured. 'I need whatever comfort I can get. And who are you to say I shouldn't have it? Or to judge me at all? Priest *manqué!*' He turned his face to the other side of the bed.

But I'd had my say. And his impersonation of pathos had had no effect.

'Get me Mikie,' he said.

I won't, I thought. This man can't do anything. He chooses the audience for his tantrums. He won't try one for the hospital authorities. 'Michael's had enough,' I said. 'He needs a break.'

He brandished the crucifix, then held it motionless. 'Mikie,' he bawled. 'Mikie!'

Michael appeared at a trot.

'Mikie, you'll stay with me, won't you? Just for a little while.'

'He doesn't need you,' I said. 'The staff will look after him better than anyone else.'

'Stay with me, Mikie,' he repeated.

Michael didn't look at either of us. He stood at the side of the bed and swivelled his hands around the guard-rail.

'We've got twenty minutes,' I said.

'I need you,' he said. 'You'll stay with me won't you?'

'Well,' said Michael, looking at his own white knuckles, 'just this once.'

A REAL LITTLE
MARRIAGE-WRECKER

I have no trouble now understanding his behaviour then. Which is no great boast. I've had twelve years to dissect it. Though in fairness to myself I think I could say I only took half that time. I had the list of his excuses made out years back. I had to compile it myself; he left, and left me without providing any. But it's a respectable list. I mean it's lengthy and plausible enough. It does me credit. I juggle the order occasionally, depending on my mood – which might range from the sardonic as far even as the tender.

I was on home ground. He wasn't. That fact had numerous ramifications. In the first place he was more lonely and hence more on the prowl than men even normally are. And he was as much a prey himself – not so much to me as to the courting rituals of Ireland. A lone, quite charming young man blundering onto the whirligig of pub and dance hall. From one to the other, one to the other – two, three nights a week. And from there to the carseat-inhibited courts proceeding to their messy consummations. He couldn't turn away from the group, or from the woman in it who had picked him up. There was nowhere else to go. The progression was inevitable. And, irresponsible as men might be, he could hardly be blamed for being unready for this country's contraception laws. Prohibited imports, and nowhere available, and him sticking out anyway with his voice – he couldn't be expected to be scouting for condoms in a country town. So it happens.

He was not on home ground; he was just passing through. He never had any intention of settling here. His life was rooted elsewhere. So irremovable a fact was this that it never presented itself to him as a question. To be pulled up short, and stranded here, with an instant wife and child, by them in fact, would have done terrible violence to his outlook and all his expectations. Maybe the psyche could have yanked itself into the new mould, but God knows what the legacy of all that would have been. A woman would have been investing in trouble.

And then again, he had no family here. I had. A mixed blessing of course, in such circumstances. But the worst of it is over soon. Once the child is born, benevolence forces its way to the surface. There may not be forgiveness, but a child of their own blood cannot be resisted; the family rallies round. But he had no one. He would imagine and feel the long-range condemnation from his own home, and it would never fade because he was the source of it himself. And the child, never seen or caressed or spoken to, would remain distant to any family of his, merely a symbol of shame and exile and blighted hopes.

It's a fair case for the defence isn't it? It admits of further riders and allows itself to be proclaimed in a variety of voices. I can shift from one to another so that no one is quite sure of my lasting attitude to the man. Even a fact apparently in his favour can be enunciated so scathingly that he is quite crucified on my irony. He is capable of playing so many roles – resident whipping boy for his sex one moment, my tragic romance the next – that he is of immense use to me.

I am fantasising of course, practising the gestures for a great act of bravado. I really can't say whether I have worked through his desertion or not. I always wonder about people who affirm they have managed such feats.

So she is eleven now and we are in the cocoon of the shortest, darkest days of the year. And he turns up. There had been no trailer of any kind: no contact, no rumours, no anonymous messages or donations. He rings from Dublin and says he is coming down. There is no stopping him. And I am curious. So I say he can come, but I do nothing more positive. I do not go to meet him nor give him directions. I merely make sure that he will arrive when the child is at school.

He is solemn when he arrives. That seems correct. There is no bonhomie, no large gestures of emotion. We do not touch, though I notice that his hands are held ready to shake mine. But I do not invite them. Hence I find that I tend to avoid his eyes. If I met them, it would be hard to avoid some kind of emotional statement, and that would be premature. As a result my manner is a little too much the aggrieved and stern elder silently letting in the delinquent for his dressing-down. But better to err this way than to gush or be frivolous. That might relax him for a moment, but he would turn uneasy, and wonder.

The conversation goes like this. (I try to keep a neutral tone.) 'This is ... ...pected surprise.' I wonder whether he is going to suggest that he just happened to be in the area.

'I've been thinking about it for a long time,' he says.

I wait. The running is all his to make.

'I owe you an apology. Saying that is totally inadequate, I know. But to go on and on, explaining and repeating myself, would be useless. And messy. I am very sorry. I really am. I panicked. And I felt helpless. I'm sorry.' That is clearly the end of his set speech. I can actually see him relax in the chair after he has made it. His strategy is obvious, but sensible enough. A comprehensive apology, no attempt at excuse. And so my guns are all spiked. But I am not thrown off balance. If I want to come back to the point, I can do so, and thereby take the upper hand, at any time.

'Well . . .' he begins, now that he feels set free, 'tell me all about yourself.'

I shrug. I still feel just too cool, and no one can launch cold into a lively, revealing response to that kind of invitation. 'What would you like to know?' Superficially the question sounds like an invitation to intimacy, but of course it is quite the opposite. I am refusing to be carefreely open with him. Let him specify what he wants to know, and I will see about accommodating him.

'Well, what are you doing? Are you working?' he tries.

I know what he means. I will ignore the gaucherie in the question. I tell him about the advantages of being a school library assistant, and how you have just enough and no more to do with the children, and how the hours suit. And he nods, and says yes, and smiles, and all the time I can see him waiting for what I don't mention. His eyes wander. But in fact there is no obvious evidence of a child. She is at that age, just past toys and not into the chaos of adolescence, where things identifiably hers are not left lying around. He seems anxious when he doesn't see anything. I realise he may hardly know a thing – whether the child was a boy or a girl, whether it's still alive, whether it lives with me or is in a home or a boarding school. He may know. He may be in touch with other people around here. But he looks anxious. I can even see him juggling and formulating his approach.

And eventually, at a moment when I am reaching down merely to scratch my ankle, he says, with a nicely calculated ambiguity, 'And the child? How are you coping with that?'

He's not really interested in my coping, I warn myself. He just wants to know about the child. So I tell him. 'She's a gas little woman, really she is. We get along famously. I can't see anything other than the Irishwoman in her.' I pause and perhaps I raise my eyebrows in just the faintest smile. 'Maybe that's a compliment to you. After all you were at home here. You seemed to acclimatise very well.' But going that far is a mistake. Referring to the old days, and then to his paternity, especially so casually, is holding out a hand far too readily. 'We're very close. Naturally enough. Not that she's spoiled. But you can go and ask other people that. She's a good child. I know I can say that. My balanced outlook is well known to everyone.' I purse my mouth and give a brief nod of the head as though defying him to contradict me. He does not know whether it is a joke or not.

'You're very lucky,' is all he says. He's uneasy, and his glances slip to the window, and try to edge round corners and penetrate outside this room, the only one he has been in. And, once, there is a sudden noise of young, running feet on the footpath outside, and far from looking round he seizes up. He adjusts, even taps his tie and moves his hand through his hair, and concentrates on controlling himself. His own child is to walk in, never before seen, eleven years of age, knowing nothing. He holds his breath in trembling and in concentration. The steps pass on down the street.

I say to him, 'She's at school now of course.'

'Oh yes, of course,' he echoes me.

'Do you have any children yourself?' I ask.

'No, I'm afraid not,' he tells me.

'But you're married now, aren't you?'

'Yes, I'm married now, but I'm afraid I've got no children.'

He controls the tone of his voice carefully, so that I pick up the note of regret. I don't see any point, or even any place for a comment. I don't want to encourage domestic or marital intimacies. If he must come on his mission of curiosity, I'll make sure we remain distant animals for him to stare at briefly and then pass on.

Then he throws me. 'I'd like to stay here,' he says.

Gentle, gentle, I tell myself. 'That might involve just a few too many explanations. She's at the age where she's more than got her wits about her. And I've only got the two bedrooms. I'm sorry.'

'Don't be sorry,' he says. 'It's my fault. I don't make myself clear. I mean that I don't intend to go home, to Australia I mean. I want to stay here with you, with you both.'

Of course I am stunned. There was no foreseeing that one. Mostly I am angered. The presumption of it! And yet the tardiness of it! But because I have kept myself under such restraint throughout the meeting, I can be fair to him even now. And there is no suggestion in his voice or his manner at all that he is doing us a favour. I can admit that. And I even notice somewhere inside me, a spurt of exhilaration that I have no power over. There is something in the prospect that excites me. I could nurse that feeling. The idea of sharing the burden, and allowing the child her ... let's call it her inheritance, there's something seductive about that. But that's not fair to the idea, to call it seductive. If I embraced it, I would not be a victim, a prey. But I stay cool. 'And why would you want to do that?'

He looks at me boldly, for the first time. 'You two are the nearest ...' and he stops himself, and starts again. 'You two are my real family. What I have at home, in Australia, is not even half the real thing.' The cynical ghost must have passed across my face. He waves his hand. 'I'm not after sympathy. There's no one who doesn't understand me.' He smiles. 'I'm not complaining, I'm not criticising, I'm not trying to jump again into the same stream. Just that this is where my child is, my only child, and this is where her mother is.'

Again I must flinch, although it is very low-key. He is aware enough to pick it up. 'That means what it says. I'm not putting you down. You don't want any declaration from me, at least not now. And there's certainly no place for mere flirtatious flattery.'

I wonder if he is goading me into some kind of romantic mood by this dismissal of any thought of it. Maybe semi-consciously, but no more than that, I decide.

'It seems to me unarguable,' he continues, 'that I should be anywhere else. Doesn't it to you? He pauses, but thankfully he doesn't wait to force me into an answer. 'Don't get me wrong. The last thing I want to do is to force myself on you. I'll get my own place. And we'll take it from there.' He opens out his left hand in one of those gestures that seems more a shrug than anything else. 'I'm being direct, and maybe over-simplifying things,' he decides to say. 'But then the funda-mental issue is very simple.'

'But your life is not your children,' I try to tell him, 'any more than they should be a woman's life.'

He frowns, impatiently. 'Who said she would be?'

'But you can't just throw up all your work at home.'

'Please, please,' he says, 'I've thought about all that, I've looked after it – and, besides, it's irrelevant to you.' He looks at me, quite searchingly, and must be confirmed in his notions, for he adds, 'I know what I'm doing. I don't want you to be feeling any of that sort of responsibility towards me. As I said, I don't want to put a burden or a pressure on you at all. Lord save us, the whole idea is to be a source of help, not the opposite.'

I am in at least two minds about all this. I am bemused by this odd species of conversion or repentance that seems to have overtaken him. And he shows too much of the fanatic's humourlessness about his whole plan. But then again, the sincerity, and the apparently unselfish terms of the offer, are attractive. What would I have to lose by accepting it? His dull earnestness would pass in time – that was never part of his personality – but the solicitude and usefulness, and maybe more, would remain.

So I make him tea while I think about this. And he comes out to the kitchen with me, and stands in the doorway easily but not over-familiarly. Yes, I think, you do the balancing trick well enough, a style of reticent charm. I'll wear that.

Then he sees the napkin ring, the christening present. With the child's name and the date of the ceremony on it. And the napkin, untidily, only just pushed into it. He puts out his hand to touch it, to pick it up, to play with it. And he sees the egg stains, and the smudges, and the long-unpolished dullness of the silver. And I can't help noticing that his mind, betrayed rather than veiled by his eyes, becomes a playground, resounding with children's business, and skips, and waywardness, and high-pitched insistent cries. But there is only one child in it, and she is doing everything for *him*. And calling to *him*. I turn away; the noise is embarrassing. I forget to warm the pot, and spoon the tea straight in. For the first time since he arrived I am upset, I have lost control. He is in love with that child, I tell myself.

'Who are the godparents?' he says. 'What second name did you give her?' He hardly pauses. 'Does she come home for lunch?'

No, I correct myself, why don't I listen to what the man is really saying? He's not in love with this daughter of mine. He's in love with a child all right, but the child has still to materialise. I can't risk its being this child of mine. I look through the kitchen window into the grey, grey day. I lower my eyes into the sink and upend the teapot. Then I turn round, and I have to hold hard behind me to the cold aluminium of the sink to restrain myself from rushing over and throwing my arms around him. But I look straight at him, and I feel for him, and he must be able to see it in my eyes. 'I'm sorry,' I say, 'I really am. But go home to your wife. You're not needed anywhere else.' And again I say I'm sorry, and it's really for speaking so harshly. But I make no further concession. I stay anchored to the sink. And, whatever else he understands, he understands that's final. And he goes.

And the warm feeling of righteous triumph leaves me glowing but quite weak. By the time she arrives home from school and I pull myself out of the chair I can admit that it was a self-indulgent exercise. But I suspect that it was a useful one for all that.

ADDENDUM TO THE FIRST FLEET JOURNALS

There is no question of our superiority over the natives. Not morally nor even in point of civilisation. I am simply making a tactical assessment. No doubt they exist in large numbers, but they have no habit at all of congregation, and no experience of cooperation. Numerically greater than ourselves they may be, but their disposition to remain in family groups leaves them already fragmented.

Secondly, we have firearms.

I have just discovered we have a further advantage. The realisation was providential. We could have given away the advantage ignorant that we had ever owned it. It has been another useful lesson in the obscurantism of our own assumptions. Certainly, in this instance, it never occurred to me to inspect myself with the eyes of the natives.

By all the standards I have hitherto encountered, the natives are the abnormal ones – bearded, naked, unperfumed. We imagine they simply see in us the reverse image of all that. It never crossed my mind that the perception of such qualities as clean-shaven and clothed involved in turn other perceptions or problems. But I recall now that the

Aztecs, seeing the Spaniards astride horses (creatures they had never encountered), presumed one single, terrifying being, part-animal, part-man. Not till one of the conquistadores fell from his mount, dislodged by their missiles, were the Aztecs' eyes opened.

In our own case I doubt that the natives' perception is so terrifying. But they are puzzled and maybe even awed. While we are conscious of the right attitude we should have towards them, they remain uncertain of their stance towards us. That situation could, with great advantage, be prolonged. I must puzzle out the requisite course of action.

Our complexions, wigs, clothes, clearly intrigue them. One feature in particular takes their fancy. They are making increasing ado about our fall-fronts; a great deal of quite disconcerting staring in that region, gestures, and bemusement alternated with much communal giggling. I took this to be merely the primitives' response to our notions of modesty. Today, however, an exploring party under my command encountered a group of natives, and my eyes were opened. With unabashed forwardness and immediacy one bold native approached one of the common seamen, and poked towards his fall-front with a club. The sailor leaped back, the watching natives hooted, but the man with the club held his ground. There were women in his own party, though at a slight distance. Talking loudly he pointed first at them, then at his own member, and finally at the seaman he had singled out. He repeated this procedure several times, but it was unnecessary, for I had firmly grasped his meaning. He wanted to know whether this object of his attentions, and indeed all of us I presume, were male or female. I was not the only person who understood. A private of marines tucked his musket under his arm, and dropped his hands to the buttons of his fall-front. Only my slightly faster perception had me ready to shout an effective prohibition. He blushed in a somewhat surly way and resumed his musket. Upon my command we all withdrew.

1.   Our garb provides a complete disguise. This raises several considerations. Tens of centuries of progress in suiting the apparel to the specific personality of the male is nullified.

Even more strange, not one of our actions, apparently, has betrayed the male in us. We have hunted, shot, parleyed, given and taken commands, acted in military order. Yet none of this behaviour has impressed upon the natives what sex we are. It has not even suggested it to them.

2.   Complete as this mystification is, it is sure to be dissipated soon. We have minimal time. It will take only one convict, sailor, marine, even officer, to loosen his fall-front, or lower his breeches within sight of one native, and the power will drop from us.

3.   This power consists, oddly, in the natives being quite unaware of our potential. Most strikingly they do not know whether they should make love to us or not.

4.   Unbuttoning, therefore, must have the effect of prohibiting advances of any intimacy.

5.   But, alternatively, would unbuttoning mean that we are extending a sign of fraternity?

6.   Conversely, as long as we keep our fall-fronts in place, does it mean that not only are we determined to retain our dominance, but that we are refusing to entertain any bond of fraternity?

7.   But, on the other hand, since when has keeping the buttons on our fall-fronts deliberately in place been equivalent to the exercise of domination? It is unlacing that strip of cloth that is generally regarded as unleashing power.

8.   But, in our case, exposure in any form can only mean loss of authority and power.

9.   The question then, is how do we minimise that loss.

10. Some form of ritual unveiling suggests itself so that the occasion becomes a revelation rather than an exposure.

11. The obvious course is to take a large party of senior officers and men to a spot frequented by the natives. To call out, in precise military fashion, a predetermined fellow of the most impressively virile proportions, and to give him a brisk order to display himself.

12. A further detail is whether he should be entirely flaccid, not entirely, or altogether otherwise.

13. An even prior question is whether the actor should be an officer or an enlisted man, or even indeed a convict. Would the occasion be demeaned by the use of a felon? Is it so unequivocally dignified and noble a moment that only a gentleman is eligible? Is there any chance of the act becoming risible – so that only some common fellow should be compromised by the indignity of it?

14. The reaction of the natives is unpredictable. We do not know whether their god is perhaps, as it were, the god of a gentle breeze rather than the god of the howling wind. They might be more affected, in the desired way, by something that we might regard as more discreet and homely.

15. If the natives are unpredictable, so too perhaps are the men under my command. If they were to be officially combed for this ideal representative – presuming we could decide on what was ideal – I do not believe I could guarantee to control their response. My strong suspicion is that they would treat the matter with great jocularity. Commands, particularly those coming down from the highest authority, cannot be treated with jocularity without weakening the tight structure of discipline I need to maintain.

16. I strongly doubt whether most of my subordinate officers could appreciate my method of operation. They would have difficulty understanding the delicacy and stylishness of approach that I see as necessary.

17.   Yet I cannot conduct the search by myself nor stage-manage the denouement on my own.

18.   To throw away this fortuitous advantage would be a tragic pity, a stern question mark against the supposed superiority of the white man. Our ingenuity and inventiveness cast into great doubt.

19.   I'll start again. The natives are unable to descry the male in us. So they treat us warily and with awe. We obtain dominance, and time.

20.   Yet my men will betray themselves, and any flawless plan to ennoble that betrayal is beyond me. When the exposure is committed, it will, to my mind, be done crudely and humiliatingly.

But then it may not appear so to the natives. Further, the sight of one man may not tell them anything about the others. I have no notion how far inductive reasoning is natural to them. The man with the wig, the man with the beard, the man with the epaulettes may all be different sexes to them.

Mystery upon mystery. The waters are muddied endlessly. And for me too. Ambiguity and multiplicity piling one upon the other. I cannot exploit it. I can only extend it. What was the problem?

21.   Tomorrow I will disembark the women. Let them go to it.

17. Yet I cannot conduct the search by myself, nor place
    trust in ... Renunciation of my own ...

18. ... already were this forbidden an image would be a
    triple prey, a sight guiding itself against this argument
    ... of the ... ... corruption and inward
    ... into itself falls.

19. ... if ever again Thou ... thyselves are unable to detour the mist
    in ... So they treat ... warily and with care. We obtain
    ... finance, and dare ...

20. ... in my mien will betray themselves once my flattery
    ... variable that betrays is beyond ... When the
    ... is committed at ... to any ... that he have cruder
    and familiarity.

    But then it may betray itself to the flatterer. I asked the
    ... of some ... may ... tell them anything about the
    others. These ... to report how far informative reasoning is
    entailed to them. I'm content with this via the ... with the
    ... ... with the qualities may all the ... believing me
    to trust.

    ... ... speech ... I'll ... ... is ... ... confess.
    And came too. And ... ... one ... another. I cannot explain it. I can only ... it. What is
    the problem?

21. ... ... I will ... ... the woman. Let them ... the
    ...

THE
VICTORIA
CROSS
OF
TIMOTHY
O'HEA

I left for Maitland two days after landing from the boat. I had damn-all time to get ready. Offhand I'd say I spent two minutes wondering what to do with the piece of metal. I thought of taking it with me; it could have been a curiosity on the way up-country; the women and girls would have been impressed. With the men it might have compensated for my recent arrival and unfamiliarity with the place. It might even have won the expedition a bit more standing, maybe a few extra supplies and offers of help. But there was as much again, or more, against this. I'm not sure that too many people out here have ever heard of the Victoria Cross. I'm not blaming them. Why should they believe it's anything but some foreign geegaw? And it's not done for me to start saying what it means. Those shy – or is it sly – withdrawn men I have encountered all the way up here, holding their distance, their heads bent, watching me from under their eyelids, they would certainly not have been impressed by any immigrant blather. No, better to do the present job, and establish new credentials here. Keep quiet till then. The medal will get its authority from whatever I manage here. That's what spreading our civilisation means. Getting whatever they come up with over there to ring true out here. I'll keep the medal till the return. It'll be a hit then.

I write to my mother once, sometimes twice, a year. Some day I'll probably go back there. A suitable sort of place for old age. Looking down the bay, out towards the west. You might see Canada on a clear day. But I've no interest in seeing Canada: too cold, and, for that one brief moment, too hot. The quiet life in Bantry with the old lady would do. By the time the only adventure and travel I'm good for is easing myself along in some old bit of a boat up and down the bay. Maybe by that time I could chew the cud of my past very well. I could become the famous old man of Bantry celebrated for his travels and for valour. I could always send the Cross home to her now. She'd appreciate my entrusting to her the one thing of value I have. Give her something to talk about to the neighbours, draw people in to see her. And it'd be a way of keeping my memory alive till I get back.

I haven't seen her since I left home. Certainly not since I won the thing. 'That's very nice, my dear,' she wrote to me. 'Is there a pension comes with it?' And that was all she's ever said. I'm worried it's the ghost of her father that's with her. Him standing on the rocks at Bantry in the Christmas of '96, steadying himself against the storm, watching the heavens lash the French fleet there in front of him, screaming out to God to wake up, and God staying asleep for six days. She was her father's daughter all right, and she cursed the storm that damned Ireland or saved Ireland or whatever it was it did to Ireland and sent Tone and his French republicans back to sit by their guillotines again. She said nothing when I took Victoria's shilling . . . but I don't know.

I trudge on across this dry but washed-out land. Neither of them, I keep thinking, would recognise it as a part of God's earth, and they are wondering what I'm doing here. The old man, or sometimes his daughter – I can't tell which – pulls me up and says, 'Where did you get this dull bit of tinsel?'

'In Canada,' I tell them.

'What for?'

'For valour,' I inform them.

'Was it Indians?' they ask.

'It wasn't,' I admit.

'I've heard of no other wars in Canada,' they say, 'not since that old toad John Bull squatted down on the place.'

'It wasn't an official war,' I tell them.

'What was it then?'

'It was troubles.'

'Who with?'

I have to hesitate. 'Some Americans,' I say, and I know that admission is bad enough.

'What sort of Americans? Runaway niggers were they? Or Jews or the like?'

'No, none of them.'

'Well who was it then?'

'Fenians,' I confess to them.

If Hume gets back, perhaps he should take the Cross. Surely the possession of it must have a sobering effect on anyone. On the recipient, of course: I don't know anything – religion, honour, love – that can compel behaviour quite so drastically. Surely even a mere guardian of it couldn't escape that compulsion entirely. It might just make the difference to Hume. If it were a dying wish surely he'd take some notice. Would think twice about staggering into every grog shop his nostrils get a whiff of. Just every third, or even every second one. If he can keep the grog a bit lower in his system he won't have the other troubles. Not till we got to Thargomindah did someone tell me the fellow was on parole. It explained a lot.

He was in charge all right; I never questioned that. He knows the country, it was his idea. But there were traces of resentment there. When he gave me orders I caught him watching me a fraction longer than he needed to. They'd recommended me to him as someone who had the decoration. He seems to have been put in two minds by that. Sure, I was suitable but I was some kind of threat and reproach to him as well. He was on the look-out for signs of mutiny, half-hoping for them because it would strip me of that authority he couldn't help investing me with. But I didn't rebel, and I said nothing to him about the horse-stealing. Perhaps that only made it worse. Him wondering whether I knew or not. And it wasn't good for the coordination of such a small, even intimately small, expedition as this.

On the last night before we left Thargomindah he took to his grog savagely. And he asked me questions. 'How many Fenians did you kill, Paddy?' he began. It was out of the blue, and surly enough; there was a grudge there and mockery, but restrained by some kind of awe.

'None,' I said.

'Ah, come on now. Aren't you supposed to mow them down for that kind of honour from Her Majesty. You know, get in among their murderous Irish throats and their poisonous Irish bellies with the bayonet?'

'I killed no one,' I repeated.

'What sort of a soldier is that?'

'Well I'm not in the army any longer, am I?' I teased him.

'Look, O'Hea,' he said, 'I'm starting to wonder whether this story is true. I've certainly never seen the fucking thing. You can't just land here, with nothing to your name, and think you'll have us all bowing and scraping at the mention of some doubtful award for an even more doubtful bit of bravery. Did you do anything or not?'

I bridled. Why, I thought, should the fellow bully me? 'You

come and see the bloody thing in Sydney,' I said. 'And the citation. You can read it all there. And it's not signed by me.'

I thought he sobered up, for just a moment. Some rarely heard voice cautioning him not to be intrusive. His next question was, for him, oblique. 'Were there many killed?' he asked.

'None.'

'The fire can't have been very heavy.'

'There was no gunfire at all.'

'What sort of fight was this? Don't tell me the British army was using bows and arrows.'

'There was no fight, there was no real war. I never so much as saw a Fenian.'

'For Christ's sake, you slippery Irishman, what was it you did?'

Oddly I felt pity for him; I had to put the fellow out of his misery. But I was uneasy too at having to give him the knowledge. 'We were guarding a train,' I told him. 'There was a wagon full of powder and ammunition. It caught fire. I was the first to notice it. I gave the alarm. I managed to find a supply of water, a bucket, and a ladder. I got the fire out.'

Hume stared at me. By the irregular light of the fire I could see the jostle of reactions on his face. Incredulity, amusement, relief, and, above all, triumph. 'You threw a bucket of water on a fire, and they gave you a medal? *The* medal!'

'Not a bucket of water at all,' I objected, and I sounded a bit pathetic even to myself. 'I had to climb that ladder seventeen times.'

'Christ,' said Hume. 'You fucking athlete. You don't get a medal for that sort of thing. You join a circus, or you repeat your trick on street corners.' And as he said this he hoisted himself up, bellowing with the greatest self-complacency. He picked up his blanket and shook it out, then laid it down again probably three feet further away from me – far enough to show his new-found disdain but still close enough to the heat of the fire.

I doubt whether there's any point in consigning the thing to him. He seems to be secure now in his contempt and his independence from me. 'I think we should fill the large water bags here before we leave Cooper's Creek,' I suggested.

'Don't be a fool,' he said with an assurance he'd never shown before. 'The whole point of a small group is so we can move quickly. You're not going to repeat your seventeen buckets here,' he said, and his laugh had a peculiarly rich pleasure to it.

I've never been to Germany. I'd hardly say I've ever met any Germans. They and their country mean nothing to me. No bond, no curiosity, no desire, nothing. They've just done for the French, got into Paris in a few weeks. Well . . . that was probably a good thing. The French have never been much use to anyone except themselves. The Germans . . . well . . . I don't know. There must be something a bit helpless about them.

In my twenty-eight years I've had two responsibilities. And they've been Germans. I've never chosen them. It's had nothing to do with me. But the moments of crisis come, and I find myself volunteered, and behind me I hear the heavy broken English and the formal addresses of relieved but unhysterical Germans.

When we meet this man he'll have reached old age. He'll speak no known language. Hume knows a little about him, but a sulky horse thief is no proper saviour for a scientist and a gentleman. Nor am I either of those. But a soldier's bearing stays with him, and the German and the soldier will hear the right echo in one another.

'Doctor Leichhardt,' I will say, 'welcome back. The Colony, and the world, will have its own way of honouring you.

But could I just mark my own meeting with you? You have been the recipient of many awards yourself. I have this medal, but in the life that I foresee I shall lead I am not sure what I could do with it. Flattered as I am to have it, it could in many ways be too much of a worry, even a burden. As far ahead, that is, as I can now see. It would be a good idea if it remained in your keeping.'

'I am honoured,' Leichhardt will say. 'But why me?'

Hume will resent all this. He will be enraged by my bond with Leichhardt but he will not dare interrupt a conversation the great man is interested in.

'If I have had any destiny at all,' I will reply, 'it seems to be that of providing safety to the German people. A court appointment almost. Not that you are anything but safe and healthy and at work. But, in the popular eye, the task of locating and returning you to civilisation is considered saving you. I apologise. I know too well it is nothing of the kind. But I cannot avoid being seen in the light of a saviour, and gaining repute and honour from it. So I owe you something. You have a right to this medal.'

'Why this?' Doctor Leichhardt will say. 'Is it a German medal?'

'It's the Victoria Cross,' I will tell him, 'an English medal.'

'You fought with us against our enemy, the French.'

'I have never fought,' I will admit to him, and for once, to this stern Prussian, I will not be hesitant to admit it. 'I put out a fire on a train. It was carrying gunpowder and ammunition. It was also carrying Germans, eight hundred of them. It was in Canada. They were travelling into a continent. To a better life. They are enjoying it now.'

Doctor Leichhardt will appreciate that.

'This medal,' I will say to him, 'the Victoria Cross, will always be a sign of the mutual succour between the German and British peoples. Between the German and the Australian peoples. And now, if you will excuse me, I must lie down. I have a feeling of great fatigue.'

Poor Hume will not like it. I have no wish to usurp any of his roles. But I have a private matter to attend to, and I believe Doctor Leichhardt would make the perfect guardian for this piece of metal that I lie awake over. It has nothing to do with Hume. When we meet Doctor Leichhardt I shall have my say, simply. Till then Hume will find me unexceptionable. When we meet Doctor Leichhardt, then . . . Poor Hume, I can see him drifting away. 'Hume,' I call to him, 'if we meet Doctor Leichhardt, you must speak to him first. I will take my turn.' I cannot hear him answer. He is drifting away.

The sharp points would have been ideal for crushing the nardoo seeds. The seeds shy out from under the thin point of my knife. The stone crushes well enough all right, but it mixes in its own grit. And it is heavy. So heavy. But the eight points of the cross are blunt enough to pinion the seeds and yet sharp enough to splay them. And it sits in the hand and I can revolve it. The cross turns and here, in these extremities, it provides sustenance. I can feel the points turning through the palm of my hand, and the hand raw, but that a minor thing, because the points of the cross are eking out sustenance. Lying back I can see the cross revolving against the sky and showering down all that I could wish for to nourish and refresh me.

The dark bronze spins, and the sun catches it, and it glistens, and the flashes of light leap down to me. From the points of the cross step the dark glistening shapes. But my eyes are going, and all I know is that they are dark shapes. I cannot see what they mean. But they must belong to the cross. Perhaps it's them I should give it to. If they are attacking me, then I yield it as a warrior to other, stronger, warriors. It is the spoils of war. And if their meaning is kindly

– and I see the dark revolving ring of bronze enclosing me –
they take whatever I can give them. And I can give them the
cross. It is at least a different kind of trinket and they will find
their own use for it.

Still the bronze spins, and the points fly off in every
direction. Everything is blurred. I feel giddy. I don't know in
which direction to step. I think the footing is there beneath
me, and I flex my leg, so faintly, just before I step off, and no,
there is nothing there before me where I can ground myself.
But I am not standing. I am lying flat on my back, and I realise
that my body is resting on a trapdoor. That if I throw my head
back any further or expand my chest as I try to take in air or
stretch out my feet for some momentary ease, then I will
upset this see-saw and the trap will spin, and I with it, out of
control into the abyss. But I am sitting, and I am part of the
bronze circle and there, on the coarse, feverish sand, are my
mother and my old commanding officer and Mr Wyndham
from Thargomindah and a queue of German immigrants and
Hume and Doctor Leichhardt, and no one sees anyone else.
And, for a moment, the bronze points are no longer there,
and I panic and the circle disappears and the bronze points
reappear as though it were because I had wished them to.

Slowly the cross stops turning. The dark, engraved, discreet face comes to rest. I address myself to it. 'We belong
together, it seems. Otherwise we belong nowhere, either of
us. You are an embarrassing and unnatural growth. And so
am I, so am I. Of much noise and little achievement. Children
of dispossession, both of us, compensated by toys.' I reach out
to the silent bronze face and pin it to my breast.

THE
ARCHBISHOP
OR THE
LADY

Twenty-one years later he came to my bed. I'm not just being archaic or coy or romantic. It is a precise description of what he did. It was late one Friday night, when the children were all asleep, but I still had the light on and was reading. I'm not casting any slur if I say that ever since I had once more become legally single he had been aware of me, in contact with me, in a way that had not been true before. He certainly always knew when I was attached or between attachments – not least because I always told him – it was that sort of intimacy. And now too it was the dying days of his own marriage. So when he turned up, unannounced, I had to restrain myself from some such operatic greeting as 'I was expecting you.' True as it might have been, it would have suggested a self-possession and control of the situation that I certainly did not feel. I had envisaged his initiative, but I had not decided on any response.

So I let him in, and the natural reaction to his apologies and protestations was to hop straight back into bed and to let him look after himself. He came and sat on the side of the bed. It served no one's purpose for him to stay there. He would have done so, at least for some time, and then only have made his moves tentatively and ambiguously. Too much the gentleman, too much the adolescent. I'm too old for that. He had played his cards quite openly by coming in the first place, and I saw no point in prevarication now.

'Why don't you hop in. You'll be much more comfortable.' I laughed and tried to give it a reassuring tone. 'And so will I.'

He undressed, to his briefs, but without any trace of emotion. No sign of haste, no sign of resignation. But as he went to the far side of bed and got in, back to me, he said, 'Actually I feel I want to have a good talk to you.'

'Fine,' I assured him, 'make yourself comfortable.' I patted him on the hand, but otherwise made no move to change my position. It was a November night, with just enough of the fresh warmth of summer in the air to key me up.

'I don't really know where to begin,' he said. 'Somehow I feel it is a season of anniversaries.'

'Ours certainly,' I admitted, thinking back to teenage courtesies, and an aesthetic restraint, and a lemon shared silently in the garden while the unrestrained children of nature moved to the chords of Buddy Holly and Duane Eddy.

'Yes, that too,' he agreed, and I could see that it had not been on his mind, or at least that he had not been allowing it any prominence.

'Do you ever get a sense of your place in history?'

'No,' I said. 'Never.' It was true. History and my life are total strangers. But it was more to the point that he wanted to talk about himself, not hear about me.

'You haven't started to grow old, that's why,' he said, and he stretched out a vague, blind hand in my direction. For the first time since his arrival there was a light touch to his voice, and so in spite of the rather tired gallantry of his remark, I responded by finding his hand and giving it a squeeze of encouragement.

'Well . . .' I said. It was enough of a demurral against any assumption that I had only the bright, forward face of the child. 'Besides, I'm not even an attendant lady. I've never so much as waited on the great. And I very much doubt whether that's been a loss at all.'

'No, of course not,' he hurried to assure me. 'Except in rare cases. Just occasionally, very occasionally I suppose, it helps you to take bearings, to get a perspective. An eminence from which measurements can be taken. Mundanity is just not a platform.'

He does nudge away in the direction of pomposity a great deal of the time. But he was getting around to whatever he wanted to say, and there was no point in pulling him up short. I felt no fatigue or unwillingness to listen. His very distance from me, his leisurely, unselfconfident preamble were atypical enough to stimulate me. I found myself putting my book away, sinking slightly into the bed, and pulling up the covers a fraction – all a gesture of settling in. But I knew that if he couldn't be bumped around he could be led. 'What is the anniversary?' I asked.

'The death of Archbishop Mannix.'

For the first time since he'd arrived I felt a twinge of relief that there was no third party eavesdropping. People who keep historical anniversaries are a tiresome, earnest, simple-minded lot. Amongst people I associate with the only anniversary commemorated is the overthrow of Whitlam – and even that illustrates all the worst features of the habit. But this midnight memory, welling up in someone I thought had a healthy scepticism about the cloth and all its works and pomps, sounded like recidivism of a most embarrassing kind. And in any case such a choice seemed so bizarre, so meaningless to me. 'Fill me in,' I asked. 'When did that happen?'

'I know, I know,' he answered, and he actually unloosened himself and turned towards me. 'It's all very idiosyncratic, but you, if anyone, would understand.'

It was not flattery. I could feel the affection, and although there was a spurt of cosy emotion behind the sudden kiss he gave me, there was certainly no planning. I put my arm around his shoulders and drew his head towards me.

'I feel . . . illuminated,' he began. 'And you know I'm not a mystical type, not even a religious type very much. It's just that the round figure of twenty years seems to be working like some kind of gong in my mind. Twenty years since I left school, twenty years since I became a novice. The year, 1963, hangs over me now. 1963 and all the promise I had. You know I had promise. Everyone knows it. That just makes the post-mortem all the more dicey. Maybe I've been trying to distract myself by asking if the year really was so significant. And the one event consistently recurs. The death of Mannix. It seems terribly significant, but I'm not sure how. I really seem to have had some sort of a revelation. In fact what convinces me it's the case is that the interpretation does not come easy. That's a revelation running true to form. It's a phenomenon of my old age. I had the experience all right back then in '63, but I never seem to have made anything of it until now.' He paused. 'You must get a lot of this sort of crap.' Then he tried to be jocular. 'But this is a mid-life crisis with a difference.'

'Stop it. It's nothing of the kind, either kind. You don't have to interpolate for me. Let's take all that as unsaid.'

For a moment I could feel the tension in his shoulders as he considered taking me up on my admonition. But he let it pass. 'No, all right,' he said, 'I'll be intimately theological. My revelation had all the classical ingredients. The circumstances were highly unusual, so that my memory was able to make special provision. I took in the detail at the time, and my imagination and brain have been able to work on it for years since. "And Mary came down from the Temple and pondered all this in her heart." '

I jabbed him lightly in the cheek with my knuckles. 'Go on, stop the drivel. Which of the saints did you see, or was it God himself?'

'They took me to meet Mannix. As part of the novices' training, we spent a month in the hospice for the dying – wiping the brows of those in their agony, laying out the dead, falling in love with the nursing aides, reciting the rosary over the PR system, gathering the wisdom and bawdry of the old. Not the common-or-garden routine of the eighteen-year-old male, but ordinary enough for all that. What made it different was that Mannix lived next door. To a Sydney boy he was a distant luminary who really belonged among the fabled dead. Suddenly he was there, next door. Every month the two novices on duty were granted half an hour with him. It was late October 1963.'

'And I was still, as always, among ordinary mortals,' I reflected. 'I was in the last years of leisure when final school exams were still a token obstacle and before the world got too much with us.'

He looked across at me. 'Yes,' he said, 'and who else is getting romantic? The indian summer before the storms came. The more conventional pattern but harder, I admit.' He reached up and stretched the skin on my face where the crows' feet stood. ' "He shall wipe away every line from their eyes." '

I half-brushed, half-slapped his hand away. 'Leave them,' I said. 'They'll be useful credentials when I go to judgement.' But I didn't want to discourage or distract the expansive mood. 'Mannix and the turning spring of '63.'

He stared ahead for a moment, apparently composing himself. 'The house . . . Raheen . . . was what came to mind years later when I first read Yeats – peacocks on the cultivated lawns. Otherwise the building was irrelevant. We were taken up to his bedroom, a slight, earnest primary school teacher from Ipswich and myself. The archbishop sat close to the grate of his fireplace, fully dressed, biretta in place, and a red tartan rug around his legs. I was awed and nervous. Of course I'd never met a dignitary, and here my very first was this eminence from the past, half in uniform, half in motley, and with the inscrutable expression and elaborately slow speech and gestures of the immensely old. He was ninety-nine as every Catholic child knew. I remember only one moment in our conversation; it is as much as I remembered at that instant, twenty years ago, when I left the mansion. Cricket must have been mentioned. The previous summer Ted Dexter's Englishmen had toured, and their manager had been the Duke of Norfolk.'

'The premier Catholic earl,' I chimed in, sensing a direction to this anecdote.

'Exactly. The premier Catholic earl,' he repeated. 'The archbishop made much the same point. He said he had met several Dukes of Norfolk in his time, and the first had been in Rome, when he was a young priest, just newly ordained. It must have been about 1890. Nearly a century ago.'

I shifted across in the bed, and snuggled, with my head on his shoulder and under his chin. He stroked my arm, but I think it was a reflex of his charm, and the rhythm of his story never changed.

'Another young Irish priest and himself had missed out on a papal audience that had been arranged. "But," said the archbishop, "in Rome at the time there happened to be a group of English Catholic pilgrims, and they were led by the then Duke of Norfolk. They themselves had a private audience arranged with His Holiness, and somehow the Duke got to hear of the plight of the two young Irish priests. He asked us if we would like to join his group." At which point the old actor paused, and exercised the decayed jaw and rolled his lips in and out on the gums. Then he said, with clearly satisfied pride, "We refused." There was a hiatus, filled only by a mild panic, as we both fought for the correct response. It was the barely vestigial Irish in us, we both decided, that was supposed to be reacting, and so we laughed, the Ipswich teacher more fulsomely, but both of us were forced and tense. We were, I suspect, just a little disedified at this tale of churlishness and Catholic fragmentation. Maybe our discomfit betrayed itself. Or maybe it was wholly predictable, and its occurrence counted on by the archbishop's strategy. Two Jesuit novices were nothing to him: he had been playing with the reaction of crowds when our grandfathers were young men. Two priggish youths were but clay. At any rate, at some carefully judged moment, Mannix leaned forward to us, to me, and his expression gave nothing away, except that I saw, or was it I imagined, or simply that I now imagine, a twinkle or perhaps a glitter in his eyes. "Ah, but you must understand," he said, with the most attentive articulation, "that the English and the Irish were not such good friends then as they are now." He hung forward an instant, then subsided into his chair, and made a minute readjustment to his biretta. The half hour was up.'

The narration stopped. But there remained a distance and solemnity about him, as though he had not really been talking to me, but had been intoning to himself, and was still listening to the last echoes die away. I lightly tugged the lobe of his ear. 'Come away, come away,' I called. 'It's a nice story, but you're in the real world now.'

'Hang on,' he said. 'I haven't made my point yet. As we walked off across the gravel towards the gate, the Ipswich teacher said, "Funny old codger. Bright as a button." I suppose I grunted some sort of assent, being a well-bred young novice, but even then I had an irritated sense that he had demeaned the man and the moment. Not that I expected him to rise to the moment: he was a colourless, unimaginative youth, and it was a pity the occasion had to be wasted on him.'

'Why are you so angry still?' I asked him.

'I'm not,' he said with tired calm. 'A bit sad perhaps.'

'Angry, sad, whatever you are, you shouldn't still be

emotionally subject to all that. Heavens, it was virtually your childhood.' I raised myself from his shoulder, and settled back on my pillow.

'Maybe, maybe, but you miss my point. Yes, I'm mildly sad at the Ipswich teacher, but, God, he wasn't responsible for his limitations – and they were circumstantial limitations too. He didn't get the point that I got, but maybe only because it was the end of his dealings with the man. But it wasn't the end for me. I'm talking about what I got out of it. In that story-telling I had seen achievement as an artifact. I had witnessed the honed perfection of a human action. There he was at ninety-nine, crafting his life and each segment of it, with total control, each cluster of gestures and speech and tone a lyric breaking free from him, like a detached balloon from a cartoon character, except that it always had dignity and nobility.'

He was straining just a little too hard, and I was roused. But I reined myself in from too sharp a tone. 'Are you sure you weren't taken in by experienced posing?'

'No! What I'm saying is that that's my feeling now.'

He seemed to me to be going round in a circle. I wasn't sure what he really wanted of me, but I imagined he didn't know that himself. I was an atmosphere – somehow the appropriate one – in which he could think aloud. That feeling was reinforced by the sheer oddity of our situation. In spite of the intimacy of it, we weren't even facing one another. There was contact, even some warmth, but the words were going out across the foot of the bed, and bouncing back to us from the white wall. We were acting out some domestic parody of Plato's Cave, and the sheer artificiality of it made me laugh. 'Go on,' I said in answer to his disturbed movement of query. I reached out, and with the back of my fingers I stroked his hair and the prickly side of his face. It was cajoling, but it was not wholly calculated.

'My point is,' he began, 'that what I had which the Ipswich teacher missed was a balancing experience. The following Sunday he went back to the novitiate and was replaced by another chap somewhat older than I was, a New Zealand dairy farmer, a rangy ironic bloke with a gentle contempt for Australia and a determination to keep his spirituality to himself. We laboured and laughed together over the dying: Mr Portelli, blind and barely articulate in English, lay in his cot and sucked on Kool Mints; Mr Hodgkinson, the father of two nuns, bellowed constantly for the pan and swore to the ward after every ordeal that all he could get was fucking wind; Mr Rayner scratched savagely at himself with nails he would let no one cut, and whimpered about his twin afflictions of dandruff and itchy balls, and all the while the cancer moved outwards. And one mid-afternoon, spreading the gospel of the Melbourne Cup – Gatum Gatum is the only winner I could name from that year to this – we got an urgent request to go next door. Did we go in through the back, through a kitchen? I can't even remember. Simply that we went upstairs with seemly religious haste. The archbishop was in the same chair, in the same spot, but the picture had been smudged violently. His biretta was on the floor beside him, and the still thick hair had been not merely displaced but blasted into rigid, misshapen tufts, and cowlicks slewed across the eyes and nose. The face was the first really grey one I had ever seen. The teeth had been removed and the head lolled and the dribble ran down onto the loosened purple stock and black soutane. We were there simply to get him into bed. The dairy farmer hardly needed me. He slid his arms around the back of the faintly panting figure and hoisted him. I was hesitant about touching this flesh, but the prospect of its being dragged must have struck me as a worse indignity. I bent and lifted each of the black-shrouded shanks up around my hips, and we shuffled towards the bed. Up went the burden, buttocks first, on to the princely expanse. Up we went after it, crawling across the first double bed other than my parents' I had ever experienced, heaving and yanking the occupant with us, till we had positioned him somewhere near the centre. The covers had not even been turned; our task had nothing to do with the restoration of life, everything to do with the restoration of dignity. We were placing him in the sanctified attitude of death. We were thanked and dismissed.'

He was silent. All the time I had not taken my hand away from the side of his face. I moved it with uneven strokes and in an irregular rhythm, determined to keep him alive to something outside his own engrossing memories. But I couldn't just ignore this focus of his concentration. 'Something to tell your grandchildren,' I said. 'Or the likes of me in the meantime.'

'Come on,' he turned to me, and propped himself on his elbow. 'You can do better than that.' And for the first time since he had arrived, I felt an engagement about him, the initial movements of a hardening towards passion. There was anger present all right, but it was the kind of spark that ran out igniting a whole web of feelings.

'Glib, insensitive responses are too much the order of most days,' he continued. 'The dairy farmer was at it too. "All in a day's work," was his only, laughing remark. And behind that, at the most, was the hackneyed convention of archbishop and Italian greengrocer coming to the same end.'

'What more did you want?'

'Silence, I suppose. I had seen the glory, and the glory had departed. In a moment, almost while my back was turned. It wasn't just life that was gone, or a known personality that had been obliterated. It was that consummation of wit and self-knowledge and irony and tone and universal understanding. It was achieved humanity that had been taken away.'

'Look,' I said. 'In fact, look at me.' He had been talking at my throat, but now he raised his eyes, and his right hand came round and rested on my shoulder. 'Why are you telling me this?'

'Isn't it obvious?'

'No, it's not. We've known one another for ages, we can take a whole world of religion and mores for granted . . . but that doesn't explain what I'm supposed to do with these memories.'

'What do you do with any work of art,' he told me, but he did have to make an effort to stop his mouth opening in a smile. 'Contemplate it. If you get any ravishing insights, pass them on to me. But please spare me criticism.' The smile was released, and the slide into skittishness, even carefreeness, carried him on to kiss me, lightly but several times across my shoulder and my neck. And he drew himself closer, and I felt that the balance of his interest had shifted. But if he had come to cast his pearls in front of me, I wanted to see them all: he no longer seemed in danger of being mesmerised by his own alleged treasures.

'Was that the end of your dealings with the great?'

For a moment I thought he was going to waive the chance to continue. He wasn't, but his tone had altered. 'No, no, the work is a triptych. Decide the order of the panels yourself.' He tapped his finger three times across my breast bone. 'The old nuns in the hospital prayed in frenzy that Dr Mannix would live to see one hundred; he didn't. I finished my stint and went home, and the same night we were all herded into a bus to go and wake the body in St Patrick's Cathedral by singing something or other – Vespers I think – from the Office of the Dead.'

'Can you sing?'

'No, of course not. I couldn't even find my place, in the book, in the procession, anything.'

'Sing me something.'

'Careful, or I'll break into psalms and spiritual songs. We got very lugubrious on them that night.'

'Let me shut my eyes a minute, and see if I can conjure up the choir boy ... Ah, he's coming, he's coming ... No, he refuses to appear. All I can see is a beast in my bed.'

He took it as a cue, and snarled, and let his fingers beat a swift tattoo on my breast, and then he withdrew as though nothing had happened, and took up his story again. 'The whole affair was a pageant, a fancydress ball: monks and friars of every skin and persuasion, purple episcopal flashes here and there, choirmasters, and masters of ceremonies scuttling up and down like sheepdogs, piping inaudible notes on their discreet reeds, calling out page references.'

'But you were being very pious and uncynical at the time, weren't you?'

'I was doing my best to be decorous, but I knew it was a fair fiasco. Jesuits were an unharmonious rabble when it came to monastic preserves such as the public antiphonal chanting of the Office. We processed in pairs – an unvarying clerical habit, the mating instinct asserting itself no doubt – and I was beside a some-time QC from Sydney, a larrikin and great fun. He was there under sufferance. He had even less voice than I, he felt a fool in a surplice, but most of all a federal election was on and he thought of Mannix merely as a political opponent.'

'Spare me,' I pleaded.

'You are in a vulnerable mood tonight.' He lunged in, his jaw open, towards my throat, and then transformed the bite so that all I felt were the lips grazing softly and closing and opening, and the light, slow-motion prancing of his tongue. I held him by the back of the head and let my hands swing to the motion of his mouth.

'You're right,' he whispered as he caressed. 'Politics were irrelevant. There we were, in this great dim cave, shouting out to one another all sorts of crazy things across the thrilling eminence of this corpse.'

'Go on,' I told him, 'what sorts of crazy things?'

'Mad things, mad things when you stop and think.'

'Don't stop and think, just tell me.'

'Over the great patrician showman, cadaverously on show, I bellowed that I would please God in the country of the living.'

'And you did?'

'I said I would stake out the land of the living, and be pleasing in it.'

'Hold me.'

'I wailed that the time of my exile had been prolonged.'

'And I answered that my soul was in deep exile.'

'You have snatched my soul from death.'

'And my eyes from tears.'

'Free my soul from evil lips.'

'And from deceitful tongues.' And then I laughed. 'Come on,' I said, 'that doesn't feel deceitful to me.' And I rolled myself around him.

'We said other things,' he tried to mumble. 'Or we should have. In all the chaos. As the notes jangled, off-key and off-tempo, in the bleating of that great mob of lost sheep.'

'Come on now.'

'And irregularly, ecstatic escapees of sound, flashing, in trajectory, across the vault. Conceived in the muddle and the discord.'

'Blowing kisses to death.'

'And our hearts rising in the dark.'

'Brimming.'

'Swelling, in the glory of death.'

'And our eyes wide at the sight.'

'Seeing the littered earth we had risen from, the sad mess we were returning to.'

Outside, dogs barked, and nearby a child stirred and cried out, and reaching through the rain of tears I took him by the hand.

MY
FATHER'S
VERSION
OF THE
NURSES'
STORY

First the war, then medicine, came between my father and myself. In my first years and his most receptive years, my father had more things to do than hang around attending to me. He went to the war, he went to the Royal College of Surgeons. I stayed behind. He had chosen his ground, and I wasn't on it, then or ever.

So now, each from the safety of his own territory, my father and I circle round one another. We don't have much time and the questions are pressing. My father wants desperately to be proud of his children. I have reservations about his criteria, but I cannot resent the wish. He is becoming less certain about this writing business. He has always thought it an amateur affair – an after-hours activity anyone should be able to do. He has been writing all his life, he says, dozens and dozens of articles in medical journals. But now I hear him say, 'My son is a writer.' Old friends and colleagues tell him when they read something I write and find it marginally comprehensible. He offers no opinion himself. But he offers me subject matter. 'Come and see this operation,' he says. 'You might like to write about it.' He holds in his hand something I have written, and gestures with it. But he comments by way of something similar that happened to himself, or by recalling his presence at some event I have mentioned. He does not engage. Not that I demand he should. His feints are quite eloquent enough. He'll come closer in his own good time, I think. He has his own approach, his own style.

He comes at me obliquely. I approach him more directly. My strongest pull is to what is most foreign to me. There are possibilities there, I tell myself. I accept his invitation to go into the operating theatre. I check with him on medical details. I quiz him on symptoms and diagnoses and prognoses.

And I ask him about the war. I have not been to war. So I wonder and wonder about it. And I badger my father terribly about his war. I envy him. Tell me about a medical war, I ask him. Make something of it, I want to tell him. It must be a great clarifier. So my endeavours converge; I probe at the man, and I stick out my finger into the maelstrom.

I don't want any of the clichés, ancient or modern, about war. I know all that, I don't need a father for it. I keep prodding him on this event or that. I hope the individual will suddenly stand forth. But it's not easy going, getting the apocalyptic story out of him. He is ready to be dry, laconic. I prompt him with a photo album, and he does his tour of duty round the south-west Pacific. In the Ramu Valley he peers at thousands of glass plates, trying to identify the malaria bacillus in swabs taken from sick troops carried out of the jungle. He is warned not to be fooled by the fly shit. In Singapore he leads Lord Louis Mountbatten on a tour of his wards in the Fourteenth Australian General Hospital, and he says, 'I am just to the left outside the picture,' or 'I am standing just beside the photographer.' So he is not recorded with royalty.

I try to nudge him further towards the centre of things. 'Was most of the work with battle casualties?' I ask.

'No,' he says, 'mostly not.' And I think he is going to leave it at that. But he begins again. 'But the worst moment was . . . I suppose you could call it that . . . battle casualties. We were waiting in Moresby. The paratroopers had taken Nadzab. We were to fly there soon, but before we went more infantry had to follow up. They were waiting in a marshalling yard at the end of the runway. A Liberator, loaded with bombs and petrol, took off. It clipped a tree, staggered, and crashed beside a company of the waiting infantrymen. They were doused in burning petrol. We worked frantically. We cleaned the skin, removed the blisters, covered with vaseline gauze. We had rows of starkly red, shiny bodies. It was a terrible thing to do in the light of what we now know. They were literally flayed alive. Every one of them died.' My father is matter of fact. He can live with that. He has never had nightmares. Medicine has advanced. And medicine will never know very much. My father must have the perfect temperament for surgery. He has not a callous nerve in his body, but no amount of putrid or flayed or mashed flesh has ever dislocated him. All right, I say, a person can live with that. The images of the inferno are never likely to dull; they are not, God help us, uncommon. Nor even necessarily unsettling. They're on vicarious offer far too readily.

So I see no alternative but to move towards the most dangerous topic. The nurses' story is potentially his best one. But it's islanded amid reefs of sentimentality. And I refuse to be taken in by the merely sentimental. It's my father's besetting sin, sentimentality. I'm determined it won't be the final fruit we harvest from his war. But he's wary too, and I wonder if it's for the same reason. 'How did you come to be involved with the nurses?' I ask.

'Oh, it's in that book there,' he says, with as much amusement as pride, and he points to the shelf. 'You can read it all there.' It's Betty Jeffrey's *White Coolies*. He gets two mentions. It says he was there 'also'. And it says he told those POW nurses there was a ward ready. That's all. But there's more to it than that. The story absorbs me, and I can't believe it's meaningless to him. And I desperately hope that, for both of us, its strength is not as a tear-jerker. I hear it again on the radio, Tim Bowden's 'Just an Ordinary Bunch of Women,' and I thank God I'm in a room by myself for I walk around trying to blink back the tears and biting my lip and barely able to restrain myself from sobbing. It's terrible. And I think, is there any way we can end that story, any way we can climax it without making the likes of the pair of us cry?

I don't want to let him build up the pathos of it. He'll give me the sinking of the *Vyner Brooke* and the machine-gunning of the survivors. So I prompt him, 'What was your part in it all at the end?'

'Oh, it was hardly more than a formality really,' he says. He seems unwilling to get started.

'Well, how did you get mixed up in it?' I try.

'I was just told to. Sam Langford, our commanding officer, told me there'd been reports of these nurses somewhere in Sumatra, and I was to locate them.' He is deliberately flat. It's not that he can't tell a story. He is simply dragging his feet, shying away from getting properly into motion.

'All the sisters attached to our C.C.S. had been among the lucky ones to escape from Singapore on the *Empire Star*. They spoke almost daily of their colleagues who had embarked on the *Vyner Brooke*. I knew so many of the names, I knew so many of the personalities. And now I was told to locate them.' My father thinks about that for a while, but doesn't say anything more about it. I'm glad. It's one of those points where the tears could well up very readily.

'We flew to Palembang. We circled twice over the runway, with its Zeros lined up on either side. The Japanese were courteous, wanted to know our business, offered us Kool cigarettes. They showed us to staff cars and drove the seven miles into the town. On the way other staff cars met us coming in the opposite direction. The officers in each case would signal to one another by twirling a sheathed sword through the window. The other car would join in behind us. We entered Palembang in a procession of ten staff cars. Japanese troops by the roadside stood at the salute.'

'It looks almost like a special disposition of providence,' I suggest.

A tremor, part puzzlement, part frown, moves across my father's face. I know he has no time for the intellectual gloss to his stories, but in his own way I think he'd agree with the point. I explain. 'I mean it was a very fitting detail that the nurses could have been liberated in such style.'

'I suppose so,' mutters my father, but without any conviction, and as though he hasn't really heard me. I wonder myself whether it isn't a silly remark, and my father accepts it only because this is a pitfallen road he is travelling down, and he'll latch on to anything to prevent him slipping into one of his own emotional holes. Hell, I rebuke myself, it's not silly. It's one feature of the story that's as valid as any other. I could even argue that this wryly ironic climax forces itself on you.

'The nurses weren't in Palembang,' says my father, as though he's suddenly remembered why he takes exception to my gloss. 'We sent out our co-pilot in one of the staff cars, south-west, further into southern Sumatra. He found them, sent word to me, and got them to Lahat where there was a small airstrip. I immediately signalled Matron Sage. She was Matron-in-Chief. She had flown up from Australia and was waiting in Singapore for word of the girls she had inducted into the army.'

My father pauses. This is one of the danger moments. He can't help milking the emotion in the story. I want to hurry him on. But then I wonder whether I'm not just damming

back the emotion for a spectacular finale, whether I'm not
nervous that he's going to dissipate it bit by bit along the way.
Beneath that, I think, I must be wondering whether he
realises the potential and proper shape of his story. No, I say
to both of us, it doesn't have to be a runaway tear-jerker. Let's
just stick to the barest facts, and see what emerges.

'What did she do?' I ask.

'She decided to leave at once to meet them. She flew into
Palembang and I was back there to meet her. She had a
mishap which I'll always remember.'

I seize on this. 'Why? What happened?'

'As her plane landed it blew a tyre. It had to be taken off,
repaired, blown-up again, and replaced. I had with me a chap
by the name of Chisholm, a sergeant, and an ex-POW. We'd
picked him up in Palembang, and I don't know whose, if
anyone's, orders he was under. But he took charge of this
repair job. He lined up twenty of the Japs and got them to
work on the hand pump. As each one tired, Chisholm gave
him a push on the arse with his boot, and the next in the
queue took over.'

Well, well, I think, here's something to deflate the story.

My father is chuckling. It seems rather distasteful to me. I
would like it to be a large comic moment, but it refuses to slip
into that shape. The picture I see is of Australian jackboots
blasting, in a great shower of sparks and stars, wizened,
malevolent, pear-shaped Japanese pygmies all over the sky.
Stock figures, a stock picture. No, that won't fit in with the
dignity of this saga. But then maybe that's all the story needs
to save it from the gross sentimentality of the likes of my
father and myself. The tears will get dried out pretty quickly
once there's this constant flicker of anthropoid little men
lining up, bending over, and being punted, tapped and drop-
kicked all over the field.

'He was remarkably gentle,' says my father. 'I don't know

what sort of life he'd had as a POW, but this way of getting his own back was heckuva mild. He was a bit of an actor, Chisholm. Being nasty to the Japs didn't seem to be in his mind at all. He only had the one old hand pump, and he just used the most efficient method he could. Nobody got hurt or worked too hard; that would have defeated the purpose of it. He just liked the experience once again, at long last, of being in charge and able to give orders. Getting his dignity back. So he posed and strutted a bit, and generally over-acted the part. But with a healthy twinkle in his eye the whole time.' My father chuckles, remembering Chisholm.

If my father insists that's the way it was, I don't see how I can make anything else out of it. I don't see how I can stop the acceleration at this point. My father seems quite happy now to go on. 'We took off as soon as the tyre had been fixed. The flight took twenty-five minutes. As the plane landed we could see a group of people sitting under an awning on the edge of the strip.'

That's good. He's very matter of fact.

'They didn't stand up. They didn't wave. There weren't very many of them. It wasn't one of those delirious, crowd-scene arrivals at all. They waited. We taxied through the long grass. We could hear it hissing against the undercarriage and over the roar of the engines and the rumble of the wheels. We wobbled to a halt. The co-pilot pushed open the door, and the ladder went down. I stepped out.'

'You stepped out first?'

'Yes.'

'Why did you step out first?'

'Heavens, boy, it was instinctive.'

'Yes, but why?'

'Because that's what you do in those sorts of circumstances. I wasn't just going through any old sort of door. Damn it all, if it's dangerous or difficult or a man can be of some use, he goes first. Doesn't he?' My father brushes aside the triviality of it.

'Yes, I suppose so.' I give up trying to direct him.

'Matron Sage got out. I stood back. I thought she should go first. And she walked . . .'

My father stood back. He thought Matron Sage should go first. I am seized by the off-hand detail. But any man of any sensitivity would have done that, I tell myself. Oh yes! I am answered. Look at the pressures he resisted without any forethought, any tensing himself. So I look at them. He is keyed up. He is first off the plane and has a head's start. He is the senior man. He has been in charge of locating and rescuing these women. He has now arrived to liberate them. He knows all the details of what to tell them, of what arrangements have been made for them. He is a doctor and they are nurses. He is a man and his instincts must prompt him to play the gallant deliverer. And he is a young man and these are young women. But my father stands back.

And Matron Sage walks towards her girls. They are wraiths, they are like the spirits in prison that Christ visited. And now at last they rise up. And the long grass opens and Matron Sage moves towards them, her daughters, and you can hear the sobs bursting through her outstretched arms. She stands there in her felt hat and her grey jacket and grey trousers and takes each of her daughters to her breast. And she asks the echoing question of those months, 'And where are the others?', and of course they give the echoing answer, 'This is all of us, Matron'. And Matron Sage and the girls stare at the incomprehensible horror and joy of it all.

And my father stands back, and tries to stand further back, but he cannot. He is forced to watch and hear everything, and he cannot get away to any other spot. He is forced to hear these words and see these faces. He does not want these tears, but he cannot escape them. They have staked out this plot. It belongs to them alone. And willy-nilly I am tied to him and

caught also. It's no good, no good at all. My father and I sit
there and cry away together. Other people falter on the edge
of the room, and go away again.